About the Book

The New Observer's Book of Stamp Collecting is for collectors of all ages. Not only complete beginners but also experienced collectors will benefit from its advice, enabling them to obtain more enjoyment from their hobby. From its beginnings in the reign of Queen Victoria, in the 1840s, stamp collecting has developed all over the world into the many faceted pastime of today.

This book looks comprehensively at the uses and kinds of stamps and their printing, design and appearance. There is help with identification and the often changing names of countries, and much other valuable and practical information.

By means of the illustrations, nearly all specially taken and with a very high proportion in colour, over 550 stamps are shown and described, together with photographs of collectors' equipment and activities.

About the Author

Anthony New, author of the old and very popular *Observer's Book of Postage Stamps* (of which 240,000 copies were sold) is an architect by profession, specializing in conservation and restoration work, particularly on churches. He has also written several books on churches, cathedrals and abbeys, illustrating them with his own photographs and drawings.

His interest in stamps was kindled over 50 years ago, and was broadened in his school days by a mathematics teacher able to communicate his enthusiasm for both subjects. Combining his interests in the arts and stamps, he has himself designed a number of stamps for Commonwealth countries.

STAMP COLLECTING

As well as the paperback *New Observers* guides, there are hardback *Observers* too, covering a wide range of topics.

NATURAL HISTORY Birds   Birds' Eggs   Wild Animals
Farm Animals   Sea Fishes   Butterflies   Larger Moths
Caterpillars   Sea and Seashore   Cats   Trees   Grasses
Cacti   Gardens   Roses   House Plants   Vegetables   Geology
Fossils

SPORT AND LEISURE Golf   Tennis   Sea Fishing   Music
Folk Song   Jazz   Big Bands   Sewing   Furniture   Architecture·   Churches

COLLECTING   Awards and Medals   Glass   Pottery and
Porcelain   Silver   Victoriana   Firearms   Kitchen Antiques

TRANSPORT   Small Craft   Canals   Vintage Cars   Classic
Cars   Manned Spaceflight   Unmanned Spaceflight

TRAVEL AND HISTORY   London   Devon and Cornwall
Cotswolds   World Atlas   European Costume   Ancient
Britain   Heraldry

The New Observer's Book of

Stamp Collecting

Anthony New

Frederick Warne

Acknowledgements

The author and publishers would like to record grateful acknowledgements for illustrations as follows: Isle of Man Philatelic Bureau (12), John Grimmer and The National Philatelic Society (13), Omniphil Ltd (10), Southgate Philatelic Society (14, 15) and Stanley Gibbons Ltd (9, 11, 104, 106, 108, 109, 111).

FREDERICK WARNE
Penguin Books Ltd, Harmondsworth, Middlesex, England
Viking Penguin Inc., 40 West 23rd Street, New York, New York 10010, U.S.A.
Penguin Books Australia Ltd, Ringwood, Victoria, Australia
Penguin Books Canada Limited, 2801 John Street, Markham, Ontario,
Canada L3R 1B4
Penguin Books (N.Z.) Ltd, 182–190 Wairau Road, Auckland 10, New Zealand

First published 1986

ISBN 0 7232 1692 4

Printed and bound in Great Britain by
William Clowes Limited,
Beccles and London

CONTENTS

STAMPS ILLUSTRATED

1. THE APPEAL OF STAMPS

a

b

c

d

e

Stamps, like coins and banknotes, are such ordinary objects in our everyday life that we take them entirely for granted and do not enquire much about them. But when postal rates change, so that a differently coloured stamp appears on ordinary letters (**a**), or when more expensive ones are needed on a parcel (**b**) or on letters to friends abroad, we begin to wonder how many values and colours there are at the post office. Or we may ask about the unwelcome 'To Pay' label on a letter presented at the door by the postman when the sender has not put on enough stamps!

More and more frequently, it seems, there are special issues, some of them for big events like a Royal Jubilee or wedding (**c**), or a sports meeting, or at Christmas, but others without any obvious purpose. Of these special stamps most people see only the lowest value, the ordinary letter-rate stamp (**d**), but usually there are higher denominations too (**e**) (intended for foreign letters) making up sets of up to five which may tell a more complete story.

Probably however it is mail from other countries, bearing completely unfamiliar stamps, which most often triggers our interest. Although stamps have an almost identical purpose in all parts of the world, it is fascinating that they differ in so many ways from one country to another (**a**, **b**, **c**, **d**); they have an appeal which can take countless forms, and for some people the interest may last a lifetime.

For many, another first source of unusual stamps is foreign travel. When we are abroad, we need stamps when writing to our friends, and it is natural to be tempted at the same time to buy as a souvenir a complete range of those on sale at the local post office. Or if friends who go abroad know our interests they may bring some back as a present (**e**, **f**, **g**). But the temptation to buy cards of mixed stamps from souvenir shops should be resisted. Their selling price is based on the cost of the labour required to sort and assemble them (plus a handsome profit for the shopkeeper), and not on the actual value of their contents, which by comparison is probably negligible.

At first the language or even a strange alphabet (**a**) may seem intriguing. Without much practice it will quickly become possible in most cases to recognize words for Postage, Republic, etc., and a country's own names for itself and its money (**b**), and then perhaps to go on to unravel the remainder of the inscriptions with the aid of a dictionary. These may include a description of the main subject of the design – a landscape, building, animal, portrait or historical scene perhaps – and possibly an explanation of the reason for the stamp's issue, which may be an event or anniversary of world-wide (**c**), national (**d**), or purely local interest (**e**).

These are some of the simplest things to be learnt from stamps. The range of other subjects is so vast that they can only be touched on here; some will be mentioned in Chapter 6, but one of the pleasures of stamp collecting that, to young and old, sets it above all other hobbies is the immense variety of knowledge they contain.

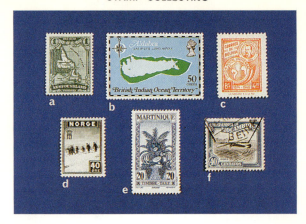

We can begin to study geography by finding countries in an atlas. Many stamps themselves depict maps (more detailed, occasionally, in spite of their small size, than those in atlases) either of countries (**a**, **b**), or to show their position on the globe (**c**). It is also possible to gain an excellent idea, from the pictures on stamps, of a country's climate (**d**), its principal industries and occupations (**157d**), kinds of export (**e**), tourist attractions (**92f**), and types of buildings and scenery. The principal towns can be identified either from pictures (**59b**) or, equally interestingly, from their actual postmarks (**f**): as a general rule the commoner the postmark the bigger the town.

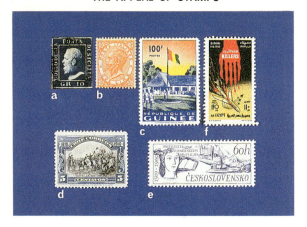

For history there are two different approaches. First, we can learn much about modern times simply by collecting the actual stamps issued in a given period. Obvious examples are the 19th century unions of Italy (**a**, **b**) and Germany from groups of small stamp-issuing kingdoms and duchies, the Russian revolution and ensuing civil war, the re-drawings of the map of Europe after both world wars, and the de-colonialization of Africa (**c**). Apart from individual stamps, original letters and envelopes (**16**) can also be found and rewardingly studied. The other approach is the study of older history from anniversary (**d**, **e**) and other special issues, though these do of course tend to be limited to events that still generate pride. It is unlikely, for example, that we could learn much from stamps about the English Civil War; however, unfriendly countries do sometimes draw attention to shady episodes of their neighbours' past purely for the sake of making political propaganda (**f**).

Propaganda of one kind or another is often found in modern stamps – in the form of political ideologies (**a**), claims to the territory of others (illustrated by maps (**b**)), advertisement of tourism (**134f**) or sports events (**152f**), or even such attempts at 'keeping up with the Joneses' as using fine London-printed stamps for showing off a newly established national airline (**c**). Then there are slogans, not only on postmarks but also on stamps themselves: 'Pay your Income Tax' (**d**) or the war-time 'Salvage Useful Materials' (**e**).

Literature is widely represented, in portraits of authors (**f**), poets and playwrights and in scenes from their works. So of course are art and architecture (**101**), though the reduction of paintings and buildings to tiny sizes is seldom an advantage and sometimes produces grotesque or unrecognizable results.

By far the biggest range, however, whilst we are still looking at the very ordinary attractions of stamps, is in the field of natural history. Ever since the 19th century birds (**a**) and animals (**b**) have been favourite subjects, and today the scope for making collections of almost anything from fish to forest trees, from mushrooms to mammoths, is quite daunting (**c, d**).

Far more important, though very little appreciated, is the highly specialized art of postage stamp design itself, which can tell almost as much about a country as the actual subjects of its stamps. Coin and medal design has for centuries been regarded as a worthy study allied to the actual process of collecting, but with stamps the subject is almost universally ignored or, at best, quickly brushed aside to make way for the technicalities of 'philately'. Indeed when designs are criticized it is far more likely to be because of some trivial or imagined slip (probably 'artist's licence' because of their tiny size) than for faults of composition or the quality of their lettering. A collection compiled strictly on the basis of artistic excellence is virtually unheard of.

These, then are some of the ways in which stamps may make their first appeal. The next chapter examines some of the ways in which our interests can be widened.

2. THE APPEAL WIDENS

8 an example of mixed mail from abroad

A few fortunate people receive enough stamps, perhaps from commercial foreign mail, to enable their collections to grow steadily and even to provide a surplus for exchange with other collectors. But however good such a source may be, they soon realize its limitations: sets will remain incomplete and older issues will be lacking altogether, and there will be growing temptations to explore the issues of other countries.

The first and obvious course is straightforward **exchanging** – uncomplicated one-for-one 'swapping' as practised by children. But that is unlikely to work once a collection is past the most elementary stage, even if the question of values is ignored. It is however perfectly possible to conduct exchanges, particularly with collectors abroad (the writer has done so for many years), provided that each partner has a reasonably constant supply of stamps to offer, and that at the start a method of accounting is agreed. As with any partnership, it only leads to trouble if either has cause to feel 'done down'.

9 a London stamp shop

A glance through any stamp collectors' **magazines** – Gibbons *Stamp Monthly* and the fortnightly *Stamp News* are good examples – will open up many other possibilities. The most obvious will be the very large number of **dealers**, to be found in every large town, and particularly in the Strand area of London. At one time most dealers sold most kinds of stamps, but it has become impossible for any of them to stock examples of more than a fraction of all those ever issued, so nearly all (ranging from single individuals to companies with dozens of staff) tend to specialize in a particular field – just as booksellers and picture dealers become known for their expertise in special subjects or periods.

10 a dealer's approval selection of Indian Convention States

   Though many dealers have retail shops, those who advertise rely mainly if not wholly on postal business, and in very many cases a considerable bond of trust and friendship exists between them and their customers – many of whom they have never met. Moreover a dealer is likely to be just as attentive to the needs of beginners as to those of advanced collectors, and for two reasons. In every collection or lot of stamps which he buys for re-sale there will always be the attractive 'plums' which he can quickly pass on to known customers whose 'wants' lists he has. But there will also be a residue (sometimes the greater part of a collection) which he can sell either stamp by stamp – a time-consuming process – or *en bloc* as a nucleus for a less-advanced collector to build on. The other reason is that beginners represent the future of the hobby and without their continuing and increasing enthusiasm its wellbeing would decline. Many dealers run a flourishing **approval** service; priced booklets of stamps are submitted to collectors by post so that selection and purchase may be made at leisure in their own homes.

11 a stamp auction in progress

In magazines will be found advertisements of **auction** houses too – ranging from the long-established internationally known names to new firms operating on a small scale, sometimes using meeting places in a succession of different towns so as to cover a wide catchment area, but in other cases relying largely or entirely on postal bids. Bidding at auction can require as much care and knowledge in the field of stamps as any other. The private buyer (and the seller too) are however to a great extent safeguarded by the fact that bidding is against dealers (who are not only looking for a profit on what they are buying but also know accurately the state of the market); yet it is perfectly possible either to secure items cheaply (if no one else happens to be interested) or conversely to be 'run up' by another bidder who is for some personal reason determined to buy regardless of market value. The principle of *'caveat emptor'* (let the buyer beware) applies as much in stamp auctions as elsewhere; one should never buy a lot without viewing it beforehand, and this is organized and encouraged by every reputable auction house. All auction rooms have a 'mystique' but for most people the fascination of the hunt and its element of chance soon overcome the fear of the unknown; incidentally there is nothing to prevent anyone attending a public auction as a sightseer, merely to get the 'feel' of the proceedings.

12 sorting and packing stamps for new issue customers at the Isle of Man Philatelic Bureau

Writing to **foreign collectors** has already been mentioned. The obtaining of new issues in this way has a particular attraction but there is the disadvantage that postal and customs delays (and in some countries a rigid official control, and in others the constant threat of pilfering) can prove disastrous. More reliable but less personal are the **new issue services** run by some dealers, who undertake to supply new stamps selected from a given list of countries, usually at a fixed percentage above face value. A middle course, possible with an increasing number of countries, is to arrange a standing order direct with the postal department or agency concerned. Of those, there is more to say later in this chapter.

13 a club meeting in progress: Children's Day at the National Philatelic Society

Then there are the **stamp clubs and societies** which, like gardening, dramatic and photographic societies, exist in every large town. Some are very long established. Most of them, like collectors' magazines, try to cater for everyone – from the very beginner to the experienced specialist – and in a well-run club each member has a lot to learn from – and at the same time to offer – the others. The principal object is indeed to offer a regular meeting place at which information, as well as stamps themselves, can be exchanged and discussed. A typical evening might include a 'bourse' period for informal business, a talk and a display of part of a collection by either a member or a visiting speaker, and a brief auction of members' surplus stamps, catalogues, etc. Some enterprising societies organize occasional visits to museums, printers and other places of interest, as well as social gatherings and public fairs and exhibitions. They also run what are generally known as club packets, which deserve a few words here.

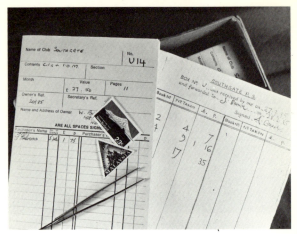

14 a club packet

Club or exchange packets are boxes containing about 20 to 30 'sheets'. Each 'sheet' is actually a blank booklet of standard page size ($13 \times 20\frac{1}{2}$ cm) with usually about 12 pages on which stamps are mounted on one side only (so as to avoid damage by rubbing or entangling). Each stamp is priced above, with possibly some identification details such as catalogue number and catalogue price. Each page is totalled in price and on the front cover are entered the value of the whole book, the name of the club, the name of the owning member, and other identifying particulars. Along with the 'sheets' is a 'postal list' which is a sequence of names and addresses to which the packet is successively passed. Each member on the circuit also fills in a form, noting the value of his purchases from each sheet, and sends this with his money to the club secretary, to whom in due course the whole packet returns. The secretary then checks it (usually a time-consuming process) and returns the now depleted sheets to their owners together with payment for sales, less a percentage commission which helps the funds of the club. Some dealers also run 'club' packets on a commercial

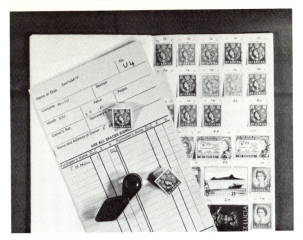

15 'sheets' from a club packet

basis, but the rising costs of postage and insurance have tended to kill those which cannot be passed by hand. The chief disadvantage of the system is that packets may arrive at inconvenient times without warning and have to be dealt with in a day or so; another, which affects the sellers, is that it takes many months to receive any takings and (unless one is exceptionally fortunate) there will be an unsold residue.

Reverting for a moment to clubs and societies, there is no doubt that they can help collectors at all levels, and not least at the more advanced stage of specializing in certain countries or groups. Such collectors are likely to find **specialist clubs** catering for people with interests similar or parallel to their own, operating on a countrywide or even international basis, exchanging stamps and information and helping one another with the answers to problems.

16 Second World War cover, sent from New Zealand to the Admiralty, London, 1941

Many collectors have no particular urge to mix with other devotees and are much happier to 'plough a lone furrow', perhaps only showing off their treasures to a few intimate friends. It is after all only a hobby and a recreation, and no one should feel compelled to collect stamps in any particular way. Nevertheless there are certain rules which may at least help to avoid mistakes of kinds that might be regretted later. These rules are in essence 'how to choose' and 'how to look after', and if we dismiss them because of ignorance or an unwillingness to 'conform', doing so may prove expensive and disappointing.

One of the 'rules' is not to take the stamps off old letters. In the early days of collecting that is exactly what nearly everyone did and, what is worse, having done so they very often trimmed the edges – and even the corners – so that the stamps would fit nicely into the spaces printed in early albums. Very few indeed bothered then about what is now called **postal history**. This involves the detailed study of postal cancellations and other markings on envelopes, and from them a knowledge of post offices, postal routes and methods of transport, and postal charges – in fact an entire facet of social history which can be closely related to the histories of commerce, of wars, of communications, or of many other subjects that may take the fancy. So an old letter or envelope left intact may have acquired

17 Brazil: pre-stamp letter, 1826

a rarity and an interest value quite unrelated to the stamps it bears; to separate them would in some cases be regarded as virtually 'criminal'! What is more, there is a vast field for collection and research in letters and markings of the times before postage stamps or even envelopes came into use, back to the posts of the 16th century and earlier. Often incorrectly called 'pre-stamp covers', they are usually folded letter-sheets.

It may be asked what is meant by an 'old' letter. Here experience alone can tell. Almost any 19th-century stamp is worth more on its original envelope. But as with antiques and buildings, date limits move forward all the time, and a fragment of history may be waiting to be told by a letter perhaps of the Balkan Wars of 1912, or of the Graf Zeppelin airship services, or more recently of the evacuation and re-settlement of Tristan da Cunha, or of Concorde flights – the list is endless but one has to be increasingly wary of 'manufactured' items produced solely to make money out of collectors, existing in hundreds if not thousands, and unlikely to retain (let alone increase) their value.

18 Morocco: first day cover, 1959

Old 'family' letters have their own tales to tell, and 'finds' in attics and old desks are still possible. Unused stamps occasionally turn up thus, but the chances are that they are too crumpled or faded to have any collecting value; moreover so far as most countries are concerned they will almost certainly have been invalidated or 'demonetized', i.e. made to be of no postal value because of their age.

Another kind of envelope is the **first day cover**. The cult for collecting these has greatly increased in many countries in the last 30 years or so, with the result that earlier ones have become much sought after. On the other hand many modern special issues with 'first day' postmarks are worth no more (some would say less) than the same stamps used separately on ordinary mail.

Another cult, commoner in Europe than in Britain, is the **maximum card**. On this the compiler tries to assemble as many allusions as possible to a single theme. For example a picture postcard of the birthplace of a composer may bear a stamp with his portrait cancelled in the same town with a pictorial postmark showing a bar of his music; if it could be signed by a descendant and addressed to a living exponent of the composer, the compiler of such an item would be particularly well satisfied. Such 'gimmicks' are not altogether confined to the world of stamps, but they show an approach to collecting which requires more effort and ingenuity than cash and provides the pleasure of the chase in a totally different way from the hunt for recognized rarities – which has more and more become the prerogative of the rich and the speculator.

A field which has become less popular than it was at the turn of the century is **postal stationery**. This term embraces all cards, envelopes, letter-sheets, wrappers etc. sold at post offices with stamps (or an equivalent) already printed on. Often the stamp design is different from that of the corresponding adhesive stamp. Collectors at one time cut them out and mounted them in albums as though they were ordinary stamps; indeed there is no reason why not, except that nowadays it is always the entire card or envelope, etc. which is regarded as the collectable item because it tells a whole story. 'Cut-outs' are useful to postmark collectors because they are likely to show a greater proportion of a complete cancellation than would appear on an ordinary loose stamp and because they can frequently be found a great deal more cheaply. Air letter forms, now known as **aerogrammes**, are now the most popular kind of postal stationery. Probably the most famous, however, were the Mulready envelopes and wrappers, issued concurrently with the Penny Black in 1840.

From the inception of the Penny Black, one of the chief worries of stamp-issuing authorities was the fear of **forgeries and fakes**. Forgeries (also called 'counterfeits') are complete imitations (**a, b**); fakes are 'doctored' stamps – for example used stamps with the cancellation removed so as to appear unused (**c**), or with the figures of value surreptitiously changed to a higher denomination. There are also plenty of examples of genuine stamps supplied with forged overprints (**d**) or surcharges (**e**) to make them appear more valuable. Little did the Post Office pioneers realize that the wiles of the forger and faker would in later years be directed far more in the direction of collectors than defrauding the revenue. It is true that **postal forgeries** have from time to time been discovered in some countries, but official methods of security printing have generally kept ahead of the processes available to the criminal. So postal forgeries (again, preferably on their original envelope) are greatly sought after, while philatelic forgeries, made to deceive collectors, are variously feared, derided and on the whole disliked. But collectors being what they are, it is not unknown for collections of forgeries to be formed for the purposes of study and research, so that consequently these items can acquire a value of their own.

If a stamp forger is to achieve any degree of success he not only has to get the design right in every detail; he also has to use the right printing process, the right colour and the right paper and gum. But it is extraordinary how many forgers, having quite convincingly overcome all those problems, have fallen down on the elementary requirement of matching the size and spacing of the perforation holes (**a**, **b**, **c**, **d**). The faker has a somewhat easier task, for he starts with a genuine stamp, and the change necessary to alter a common one into an apparent rarity may be quite minor. The amount of painstaking work sometimes undertaken can however be astonishing. A well-known trick concerns early stamps of certain countries which were issued first imperforate (without perforations, so that they had to be cut apart with scissors), and subsequently perforated. The faker buys a damaged copy of the cheaper, perforated stamp, cuts off the perforated edges, and adds plain wide ones (**e**) – so skilfully that they may only be detectable under an ultra-violet lamp.

Another danger is the **facsimile** (**a**). The subtle difference between forgeries and facsimiles is that the latter are not meant to deceive. They are produced, sometimes officially, to enable collectors to fill gaps otherwise beyond their means, and sometimes they are even marked 'facsimile' in minute letters (**c**). But once out of the hands of the original purchaser they can be used to deceive others. Facsimiles may be 'privately' produced by dealers or by philatelic societies and are sometimes contained in souvenir sheets sold at exhibitions for fund-raising purposes (**b**); from such sheets they can be cut out and offered as 'originals' even though they probably differ noticeably in paper, perforation or other particulars.

But the beginner need not be frightened of fakes and forgeries. Before he ever meets one he will see thousands of good stamps. He will probably first encounter them when he is offered an old collection at what appears to be a cheap price — but only *apparently* cheap because one or two of the older stamps in it are perhaps not what they seem. He may also meet them offered individually by small dealers, very much more likely through ignorance than by intention. The 'ignorance' when questioned may turn out to be some shade of doubt, and because of that doubt the item will have been priced low. But however low, if it is 'bad' it cannot be low enough. So once again, *caveat emptor*, let the buyer be wary and consult an expert before parting with good money. The vast majority of dealers are honest and knowledgeable and will back their sales with a guarantee, but no one can know all about every stamp that exists.

   Almost – but not quite – in the same category as fakes and
forgeries are **reprints**. As the name suggests, these are stamps
produced from the original plates or dies by, or with the
connivance of, the authorities purely in order to satisfy a demand
from collectors. Usually they can be distinguished from the
issued stamps by their paper or colours (**a**, **b**, **d**), by an overprint
(**c**) or even by a deliberate difference in the design (**f**), and
usually they are worth less. As with books, the word 'reprint'
may merely mean a second printing made to satisfy a demand,
in this case a postal one, and again there may be distinguishing
features. So the term is not necessarily derogatory. The word
remainders however is. Again, as in the book trade, it implies
disposal of surplus stock at a low price – obviously harmful to
those who originally bought at full price, particularly as (unlike
reprints) there is no means of distinguishing uncancelled
remainders (**e**). Postal authorities who indulge in this practice
(a tempting one in small countries where the nominal value of
unsold stamps may represent a very considerable sum in
revenue) quickly find that collectors will fight shy of buying
their stamps thereafter for fear of the same thing happening
again (**g**). And collectors have long memories, for such misdeeds
are recorded in the catalogues for ever!

Another practice of smaller postal administrations, aimed at collectors but deprecated by collectors themselves, is **cancelling-to-order**. CTO stamps, as they are called, come about in some cases because there is insufficient postal business (as in very small countries (**a**)) to generate enough genuinely used ones to satisfy collectors' demands, and in others because extra revenue can be had by selling ready-cancelled stamps (especially of higher denominations and sometimes remainders) – sometimes at less than the prices charged for unused. As a general rule CTO cancellations can be distinguished and are neater than genuine postmarks, and stamps bearing them are of less value. Often they have full gum. Some countries, however, take care to make them virtually indistinguishable, and if some are sold cheaply it can have the effect of making the entire country unpopular with collectors – so that what is intended to increase revenue quickly rebounds with a reverse effect, which is surprisingly permanent (**b**). Yet the dividing line between the 'goodies' and 'baddies' is remarkably tenuous, and many collectors turn a blind eye to the fact that their 'fine used' stamps of favourite countries were once part of complete sheets carefully cancelled in twos or fours (so as to make a neat semicircle or quadrant on each stamp), then washed to remove the gum, and then separated (**c**). The only difference from stamps that have passed through the post is that they are more presentable and less likely to be damaged.

Several controversial topics of that kind may be encountered. Another is the **miniature sheet**. With these, collectors have a sort of love-hate relationship. Originally and still largely produced as souvenirs of stamp exhibitions, they consist of anything from one to about a dozen stamps, either of one or two kinds or (more often) all different, specially printed together, with a margin around. They first appeared in the 1920s. In the 1930s some catalogue publishers 'banned' them. But you cannot kill a parasite by pretending it does not exist, and a decade later back they came, the older ones at greatly enhanced prices and the newer increasingly prolific. Even the British post office, once notably one of the most resistant of all to such intrusions into their everyday business of carrying the mails, has succumbed. Most collectors have however by now given up the notion of buying miniature sheets for the sake of their attractive appearance and potential scarcity value, and give money for them only grudgingly because they have to in order to achieve their aim of completeness. Many indeed give up collecting their most favoured countries when they persist in issuing too many money-catchers of this kind.

The exploitation of collectors or, as they would undoubtedly prefer to put it less cynically, the promotion of the sale of stamps to collectors, is aided and abetted by agencies. Some are merely post office departments or dealers acting on their behalf; others are big-business organizations acting in support of groups of smaller states with limited resources, and handling every stage from the suggesting of subjects and commissioning of designers to the actual sale of first day covers and the arrangement of advertising matter.

There has been a phase, which many people fervently hope has passed, when agencies – and others – seemed to be constantly racking their brains for wilder and more ludicrous gimmicks in connection with stamps. There are 'self-adhesives' (**51c**) (excused on the grounds of tropical use in places like Sierra Leone and Tonga); circular stamps individually embossed on tinfoil like giant milk bottle tops (**a**, **94d**); stamps on multi-layered plastic producing a three-dimensional effect (**b**); and even stamps from Bhutan in the form of miniature gramophone records which can actually be played!

But apart from the excesses just described, there are and have been innumerable other novelties, intended to attract attention (and, in many instances, cash). The earliest, perhaps, was the triangular shape adopted for the stamps of the Cape of Good Hope, so it is said, to enable illiterate sorters to distinguish local mail from that from abroad (**a**). That was nothing to do with collectors. However, commercially minded post offices were to discover later in the 19th century that collectors rather liked the shape (**b**). Plenty of other possibilities have been explored (**c**, **d**), departing more and more from the small plain rectangle that was chosen as ideal for the Penny Black and is still used almost universally for everyday issues. The notion of alternating two designs in the sheet (in some instances themselves triangular) has for instance developed into the spreading of a single design or pattern over two or more stamps (**e**), the repeating of groups of four or five or more designs (sometimes even of different denominations) within one sheet, and ultimately the use of a different design – all of them on the same theme – for every stamp on the sheet, as was done by the USA in a series of flags of the states and another of birds and flowers. To issue a set of

perhaps four stamps, printed in ordinary sheets, accompanied by a miniature sheet containing a specimen of all four, is now common practice. Not infrequently however the miniature sheet stamps are deliberately made different – perforated to a different gauge, or not perforated at all, or given a different watermark, or made larger or smaller. Or the miniature sheet may merely contain one stamp, the highest denomination, which of course has to be purchased to complete the set.

Plenty of other ideas have been, and no doubt will be evolved, but enough has been said to make it clear that stamps tend to divide themselves into two main groups – the pure postage labels performing the function of receipts for the cost of conveying a letter of packet, and their often highly coloured cousins which only do a useful job on rare occasions and may never even have visited the country whose name they bear. Yet the dividing line between the the two becomes more indefinite every year as more and more small states try to increase their income in this way while the bigger ones recognize the propaganda value of producing – and using in large quantities – stamps of equal fascination and often far greater aesthetic merit.

Apart from legitimate government issues, already far too numerous, there are vast numbers of 'fringe' stamps. The most obvious are **locals** (**a**, **b**, **c**, **d**, **e**, **f**, **g**), which at the outset were perfectly respectable stamps intended for limited use on certain sea and land routes, without being valid for onward transmission to other countries. In fact until the Universal Postal Union came into being in 1874, all stamps could be said to be locals, because where there were no specific postal agreements between one country and another letters had to be re-stamped – or additional postage otherwise paid – at each stage of an international journey. Some famous 'locals' like the Lady McLeod stamp issued for the ship of that name plying between Port of Spain and San Fernando in Trinidad, have become enshrined in the catalogue. Most however, even 'classics' like the Zemstvos of Russia and the famous 19th century messengers' stamps of the Oxford colleges, can only be found in special lists. At the present day there is a certain need for local stamps for places like Lundy Island, which has a few residents, many visitors and no official post office; the alternative term 'local carriage labels' is

appropriate enough in such instances (**a**). Unfortunately a few commercially minded persons, not content with dealing in real stamps, have no qualms about printing their own and inscribing them with the names of islands whose population consists at the most of a few sheep – or even of places that do not exist at all. People are of course perfectly entitled to collect what they like, but these are labels which have no place in any book on stamps, and it is regrettable that some stamp dealers choose to advertise and sell them. Rather similarly, **postal strikes** give rise to labels semi-legitimately issued by messenger services (**b**, **c**), and in their wake come greater numbers produced solely for collectors gullible enough to buy them.

Some **bogus stamps** are quite subtle, and can consist of imaginary denominations added to a genuine series, or stamps in changed colours, or genuine stamps overprinted 'privately'. There is a more definite following for so-called 'Cinderella' issues which include, for example, stamp exhibition souvenir labels (**a**), registration and air mail labels, unofficial air labels (**b**), charity labels (**c**) (such as those issued at Christmas) and even Post Office training school stamps, as well as any or all of the non-postals mentioned in Chapter 4 – anything in fact that borders on real postage stamps but is not listed in any normal catalogue. The term **forerunners** is used for labels (**e**) which precede governmental stamps for a territory; generally these are either propaganda stickers (**d**) (often of a political nature) or merely local carriage labels such as the numerous 'issues' of Alderney before its own postal administration was set up.

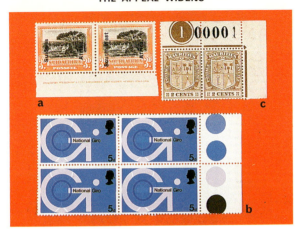

Let us return to real stamps. There is a special fascination in complete **sheets** or large **blocks**, and some collectors make a point of collecting blocks of four (2 × 2) (**39a**, **b**) so as to show clearly the perforation holes in both directions and the distances apart of the stamps on the sheet (factors which are known to vary in different printings of the same stamp). Whole sheets (called 'counter' sheets from their method of sale) nearly always have markings in the margin such as: (a) the printers' name or 'imprint' (**a**, **43c**); (b) the printing plate or cylinder number (or numbers in the case of multi-coloured stamps); (c) 'control' numbers (**92b**), 'millésimes' or similar markings indicating the year of printing; (d) guide spots of colour for the purpose of checking the quality and completeness of printing (popularly called 'traffic lights' (**b**)); (e) a serial number of the sheet (**c**); (f) indications of the values of rows or columns to assist counter clerks; and (g) probably other markings and holes to assist accurate registration of colours and subsequent perforation. Some sheets are divided into two or more 'panes' with 'gutter margins', usually of plain labels, between the panes (**43c**, **d**).

Obviously it is impracticable to collect whole sheets because of the expense and the problem of storage, but collectors can and do collect imprint blocks, plate number and control blocks, 'traffic light' blocks, and gutter pairs or blocks showing stamps separated by gutter margins. If a particular stamp has been printed by different firms or by the same firm from different plates, the specialist collector likes to have such blocks to prove it.

In many countries stamps are sold in booklets as well as from sheets. For convenience these often have two or more values joined together, usually in combinations that make up a round figure for ease of sale. Different stamps joined together are referred to as **se-tenant**. Stamps joined together but one

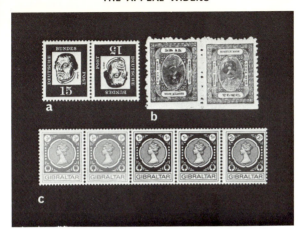

upside-down in relation to the other are called **tête-bêche**. These usually come from booklet printings in which one half of a sheet is deliberately printed upside-down so as to produce a margin at the left of every pane; the two halves are then separated and each is divided into panes of booklet size. Such *tête-bêche* pairs are intended always to be cut apart by the printers, but occasionally through an error in cutting or folding they exist still joined. To guard against illicit dealings, or merely to use up stocks, uncut sheets are sold by some authorities to please collectors (**a**). Occasionally, too, sheets are printed this way for other reasons (**b**). Much more rarely, *tete-bêche* pairs can also occur when a single unit of a printing plate is inserted upside-down.

There are also rolls or **coils** of stamps, printed continuously in single rows of perhaps 500. Sometimes they contain different denominations *se-tenant* (**c**).

Overprints and surcharges have slightly differing meanings among collectors. Overprints, as the name suggests, comprise additional matter printed on to a stamp after its original production. There is a wide variety of possible reasons: the obliteration of a deposed monarch's head (**a**, **b**); the temporary use of one country's stamps in another (**c**, **d**); even the celebration of a football victory (**e**). Whatever the reason, it usually suggests either haste or a temporary stopgap (**f**), and many such stamps are termed 'provisionals'.

Surcharges are a particular kind of overprint that changes the face value of a stamp. These, too, are usually provisionals, resulting from either a change in postal rates causing an increased demand for a certain denomination (**a**, **b**), or a delay in obtaining normal supplies from printers. Sometimes, however, surcharges are merely a way of using up old stocks of unwanted denominations (**c**), either to save money or for no other reason than to create new varieties for collectors (**d**).

Another kind of added marking consists of perforated letters or other devices. This may indicate postage due (**e**) or official use (**f**), but most frequently it is done by firms (**g**) or government offices (**h**) as a control against illegal sale or use for private purposes. Such stamps are known as **perfins** and although normally worth less, have their own devotees amongst collectors.

3. THE SPECIALIST'S VIEW

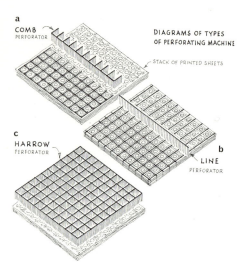

a
COMB
PERFORATOR

DIAGRAMS OF TYPES
OF PERFORATING MACHINE

STACK OF PRINTED SHEETS

c
HARROW
PERFORATOR

LINE
PERFORATOR
b

As mentioned in Chapter 2, many stamp collectors find more to interest them than mere designs and colours. Some indeed go to what others regard as extremes, to what can amount to scientific analysis. This chapter will steer a middle course, through the kinds of technicality that are known – but not necessarily followed – by the ordinary collector who has progressed beyond the 'face-different' stage of 'simplified' catalogue listings and is on his way to becoming a philatelist.

Perforation has been touched on already. The earliest stamps were imperforate but methods were soon invented whereby the spaces between them could be weakened enough for easy neat separation when required. This is done either with

rows of holes (perforation) or rows of cuts not removing any paper (rouletting). Perforation has hardly changed in its general principles since it first came into full use on British stamps in 1854, and the nature of the process, with sharp metal punches in accurate rows, has always influenced both the speed of stamp production and the standardization of stamp sizes. Most perforation is done with a 'comb' machine which punches an entire horizontal row of holes and a complete series of short rows of vertical holes simultaneously and deals thus in turn with each row of the sheet (**38a**, **39a**). Occasionally 'harrow' machines are used; they perforate several rows of stamps at a time (**38c**). If stamps in a succession of different sizes have to be perforated, 'line' machines may be used – obviously more laborious because the sheet (or pile of sheets) has to be passed through twice (**38b**, **39b**). Comb and line perforations can easily be distinguished even on single stamps by the appearance of the corners, which are regular in the latter from the positioning of a hole exactly at each corner. If line perforating is done on two or more distinguishably different machines the result is called 'compound' perforation (**c**), though the fact is sometimes disguised by 'blind' holes (**d**).

Rouletting is not much used, but it takes various forms, some of them devised so that a separated stamp appears at first glance to be perforated (**a**), whereas others produce a neat straight edge (**b**). The disadvantage of the latter is that sheets fall apart much too readily. The famous 'serpentine' roulettes of Finland (1860–75) erred the other way, with the result that complete stamps perfect on all sides are quite rare (**d**). In primitive instances attempts have been made to 'print' the rouletting with stamps themselves (**c**). Pin-perforating, so called, is really a kind of rouletting because it removes no paper (**e**).

Collectors measure the fineness of perforations by counting the number of holes in 2 centimetres. This seemingly arbitrary standard was probably arrived at to avoid fractional measurements; for instance 14 or 15 holes in 2 cm were clearly indicative of different machines, whereas $14\frac{1}{2}$ was thought to suggest a degree of accuracy that did not exist. However, quarters and even tenths are sometimes used nowadays to distinguish one printing from another – though ordinary catalogues seldom go further than halves. The coarser the gauge the bigger the holes, but it is not customary to measure the hole sizes. 12 or 14 holes to 2 cm are usual. 18 is probably the finest ever used, and 7 or 8 is regarded as very coarse. The gauge in one direction is often slightly different

from that in the other. This is because most paper has a slight 'grain' in the direction of its length and tears less readily across its fibres; it is not necessarily 'compound', since it may be from a single comb machine. In some issues of, for example, Austria and North Borneo, collectors can, approximately, date the printing of a stamp by measuring its perforation. The actual measuring is normally done by trial and error by means of a card or transparent gauge marked with dots or lines.

Variations from straightforward perforation often occur on stamps printed in coils or rolls instead of sheets. In Swedish (**a**) and U.S. (**b**) coils, for example, either the sides or the top and bottom are left imperforate; a single stamp from such a coil is described as Perf. × Imperf. or vice versa, the first description always referring to the top and bottom and the second to the sides. In some Australian coil stamps of around 1950 (**c**) the sides were perforated normally but the two outer holes at each end, top and bottom, were made smaller to prevent the stamps parting too easily; conversely some of the Netherlands of around 1930 (**d**) had a few holes omitted altogether for the same reason, and some of Ireland had merely one hole at the top (**e**).

Booklet pages or 'panes' in some countries are imperforate around the edges, so that stamps may be found with one or two sides straight-edged. At one time the same applied to whole counter sheets in Canada (**a**) and the USA (**b**); most collectors dislike border stamps from such sheets, though some try to collect all nine permutations – the four corner stamps, one from each side, and a fully perforated one from the main part of the sheet – so as to build up a kind of 'miniature sheet'.

Gutters, separating the panes of stamps within the sheet, are nowadays perforated both sides so as to produce only normal-sized stamps (**c**), but in many 19th-century British issues they were only perforated once, down their centre, with the result that stamps adjoining the gutter have wider margins, called 'wing margins' (**d**). These, although scarcer, have always been less popular with collectors, who at one time used to cut them off to make the stamps fit the spaces in their printed albums (**e**).

On many occasions stamps have been bisected (usually diagonally), with or without official authority, so as to halve their postal value. They are then called **bisects**. Obviously such a practice is open to abuse, since a cancelled stamp may be clear of the postmark on one half. However it is usually only an emergency measure, during a shortage lasting a day or two. If there is more time, stamps can be perforated through the middle and both halves officially surcharged with a new value (**a**). Bisected stamps genuinely used should of course be left on the original envelope (**b**), for a loose half stamp can be produced by anyone and so is valueless. There have been instances of third or even quarter stamps being tolerated, and some issues of the old German states (**c**) and Spain were actually designed and printed in such a way that they could readily be divided into four as an alternative to using the whole stamp – according to the rate of postage required.

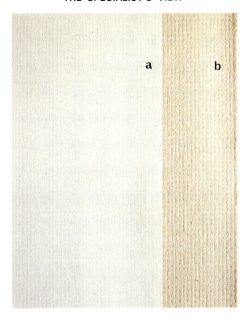

Paper, which is after all the principal ingredient of a stamp, receives comparatively little attention from collectors except in one respect: watermarks. The **watermark** is a pattern, inscription or other device produced during the formation of paper from pulp by impressing metal units which cause its thickness to vary. The most elementary form is the pattern of close horizontal lines on 'laid' paper (**a**) (such as is used in better quality writing pads, and only rarely for stamps). By far the commonest paper is 'wove', a distinguishing feature of which (by no means always evident) is a fine mesh (**b**). Either laid or

DIAGRAMS OF STAMP SHEETS SHOWING DIFFERENT TYPES OF WATERMARK

a 'SHEET' WATERMARK – LEAVING MANY STAMPS WITHOUT WATERMARK

b 'SINGLE' WATERMARK WITH AN IDENTICAL DEVICE ON EACH STAMP

c 'MULTIPLE' OR CONTINUOUS WATERMARK SUITABLE FOR ANY SIZE OF STAMP OR SHEET

wove can have a watermark superimposed. This can be a 'sheet' watermark in which a single feature (usually the maker's name and/or emblem) covers the whole sheet, so that only a small part – or in some cases nothing at all – appears on each stamp (**a**), or a 'single' watermark arranged so that one unit comes exactly on each stamp (**b**), or a 'multiple' watermark in which a repeated pattern extends all over like that of wallpaper (**c**). Single watermarks were used throughout the 19th century, but when stamps began to be more varied in shape and size they became impracticable. Repeating ones were therefore adopted almost universally so that the relationship of stamp to watermark ceased to matter. However, the use of watermarks is nowadays on the decline.

From what has been said about stamp booklet printing in the last chapter it will be seen that stamps printed upside-down in relation to others will have their watermark inverted. Thus when British stamps had watermarks (until 1967) exactly 50% of those booklets had it upside-down. Stamps in ordinary sheets seldom have it inverted, except in error or in rare cases where paper is deliberately fed into the press in a reverse direction for technical reasons. Stamps with sideways watermark may be from coils printed for delivery in that direction from certain types of machine, or they may result merely from the optimum relationship of stamp shape and printing plate to the available paper.

THE SPECIALIST'S VIEW

Watermarks are primarily a security device, firstly to aid identification of paper and prevent its misuse before printing, and secondly to guard against forging of actual stamps. Apart from changes from single to multiple, there are many cases of different watermarks being used during the currency of a single issue, and collectors consider it important to identify them. Usually this is easy, but it can be extremely difficult. The following methods should be tried in succession: (1) hold the stamp against a strong light, either way round; (2) place it face downwards on a dark surface; (3) hold it obliquely in front of a light in such a way that the light glances off the face at an acute angle (this sometimes enables the watermark of the stamp on an envelope to be identified without removing it); (4) again with face down on a dark surface, let a drop of benzine fall on it, and the watermark is almost certain to show before it harmlessly evaporates. Special detectors can be obtained which incorporate a bright light and a series of coloured filters, one of which by trial and error may be found effective in cancelling out the printed design sufficiently to let the watermark show more clearly. Before attempting any or all of these methods it is helpful to discover from a catalogue what the possible watermarks look like; if a single letter or other small piece can be identified the rest usually falls into place. Also it may be a simple matter of 'watermark' or 'no watermark', in which case any detailed identification is unnecessary.

'Impressed' watermarks are not true watermarks at all, but are applied by a metal die *after* manufacture. Imitation watermarks also exist, printed on the backs of stamps as a stopgap during a shortage of watermarked paper.

47 printed 'mock-watermark' on the back of a New Zealand stamp, 1925

Papers of many different thicknesses can be met – from the thinnest tissues used for early stamps of Taiwan (**a**) and other Asian countries, to the thin card on which certain World War I stamps of Russia (**b**) were printed in order that they could also serve as currency. Sometimes, as in Latvia, the backs of old maps (**c**) or banknotes have been used. **Pelure** paper is extremely thin, like India paper as used for books, and very strong. **Granite** paper has a multitude of coloured fibres in its texture, hardly visible to the naked eye (**d**). Coloured papers of many kinds (usually coloured right through but sometimes on the surface only) give a distinctive appearance (**e**), and have been used where the variety of printing ink colours is limited. **Chalky** paper (**f**) has, as its name suggests, a very smooth white surface; it can be identified by touching it with a piece of silver,

which leaves an indelible mark (of course this should be done with the very greatest care, and only on the sheet margin if the stamp is unused). **Enamel** paper (**a**) looks rather like chalky but does not react to the silver test, and there are others even glossier (**b**). In some cases specially surfaced papers have a dual purpose – to improve the quality of printing and to prevent fraudulent removal of cancellations. **Quadrillé** paper (found on some older French stamps (**c**)) has a mesh pattern on the surface. Some modern issues have a semi-invisible 'security' pattern on the paper (**d**), serving a similar purpose to a watermark, and a few older ones a silk thread embedded in each stamp (**e**), as found in bank notes. There are also stamps on metallic surfaced papers (**f**).

The markings associated with automatic letter-sorting and cancelling machines are generally separately printed, rather than incorporated into the actual paper, but can conveniently be mentioned at this point. Their purpose is two-fold: to 'face' letters correctly so that they pass through the machines the right way round, and to separate mail of two different classes. The first function, the facing, is triggered off by a 'phosphor'-treated or partially treated surface (sometimes called phosphor 'tag') on the stamp, while the sorting is done by differently 'tagged' stamps on the two classes of mail – that for first-class having an all-over treated surface (or in many cases two lines of phosphor (**a**)) and that for second-class only a single band (**b**) – the smaller 'impulse' that this gives being sufficient to divert the letter into a different 'stream'. This is not the place to discuss the technicalities involved, such as the chemical compositions of coatings or the wavelengths of the rays to which they react. Suffice it to say that there has been a continuous history of experiment since 1957 when black graphite 'naphthadag' lines first appeared on the backs of low-value British stamps (**c**) sold in the Southampton area. Naturally specialist collectors take a considerable interest in these variations, and some go to great lengths with the use of scientific equipment. The ordinary collector need not concern himself at all if these things do not

interest him. Catalogue listings do however often include mention of phosphor lines, which can be distinguished by the same method (3) already mentioned for watermarks, that is by allowing oblique light to be reflected on the surface. It usually needs special equipment to distinguish a stamp treated all over from one not treated at all, but the necessity need not bother the ordinary collector.

Gum, too, has received more attention in recent years, and is another specialized subject. Old-fashioned gum arabic has been largely replaced by various compounds which serve the same purpose and possess improved resistance to curling and accidental sticking. Some of these adhesives are deceptively invisible, being matt and white, but a slight colour and gloss are usually added artificially. All are activated by moisture. Though the gum on many older stamps actually damages them – usually by shrinking and cracking and so causing the paper to split (**a**) – collectors still regard an unused specimen without gum as imperfect. Stamps issued without gum are usually the result of shortage of materials, as in China in the 1940s (**b**). The problem of tropical humidity seems never to have been of great concern, and the **self-adhesives** issued by Sierra Leone in 1964, and subsequently by a number of other countries (**c**), were as much a publicity measure as a necessity.

Apart from paper and gum, the only other component of most stamps is **ink**. The occasional use of other materials – metallic foils and plastics are the principal ones – will be mentioned in chapter 5 when printing is considered in more detail. The chief interest of ink to collectors is its colour, but a secondary consideration is whether it is 'fast' or 'fugitive'. Fast ink is to a considerable degree unaffected by water, light and other influences. Most stamps are printed with ink of that type, but there have been periods (for example in Britain in the late 19th century) when the fear of fakes and forgeries has dictated the use of fugitive inks which partly dissolve or change colour when wetted. The principal fugitive colours were green and purple, and the entire 'Jubilee' issue of 1887 (**48e**, **52a**) (as well as most stamps of the colonies (**b**)) were printed in one or the other, or in one of them in combination with a fast colour (for example purple and blue, or purple on red paper). It need hardly be said that stamps so printed are rendered practically valueless when affected by water, and this unfortunately applies to a large proportion of copies of the later Victorian stamps of Britain which are met with (they change to a wishy-washy tint when wetted (**c**)) and even to certain more modern issues (**d**).

The term **shades** refers to slight variations in colour, such as occur from time to time in successive printings of a stamp (**e**–**i**).

Fluorescent inks do not seem to have been used much, if at all, for stamps, but references will sometimes be found to *aniline* colours which are bright ones, usually reds (**a**), derived from coal-tar products, and which tend to penetrate the paper.

The inks used for cancellations are worth a mention. The Penny Blacks required a red obliteration (**b**), to be effective; but the stamp colour was soon changed to red, so that black became usual for cancellations (**c**) though other colours were tried at various times either experimentally or for expediency. Mauve cancellations often (but by no means always) denote non-postal use (**d**), and they, like stamps themselves in similar colours, tend to run in water. Whilst on this subject it should be borne in mind that the inks on envelopes, particularly the red and blue stripes on the lightweight air mail kind, are also often fugitive, and can spoil used stamps by wet contact; similarly the intense colouring matter in some envelopes and wrapping paper can transfer itself to stamps and, having done so, become surprisingly immovable.

The ink of older stamps is sometimes found to be oxidized, particularly red stamps, which go dark and slightly iridescent (**e**). The effect can usually be removed with peroxide of hydrogen, which should be applied in dilute form and very circumspectly.

STAMP COLLECTING

54a Hungary: artist's engraved design for Bolshevist issue, 1919
   b Hungary: issued 60 filler stamp based on above design

As the collection of a particular country fills up, your interests can turn to all kinds of subsidiary material. Enormous fascination is for example offered by the sequence which precedes the finished stamp: artists' drawings, essays, proofs and 'specimens'. It may surprise the non-collector that such items are obtainable at all. It is likely that the great majority on the market or in private hands were acquired at best 'by favour' and in the worst cases by underhand or even criminal subterfuges within printing works. Some collectors' acute appetite for such things unfortunately fosters such practices, and the stringent security measures required of stamp printers have to extend well beyond the field of stamps themselves. Much of this kind of material is however of older vintage, and of perfectly legitimate origin – as for example from the archives of printers who have ceased business. There are strong arguments in favour of all unique items – original drawings, officially approved proofs, engraved dies and so forth – being lodged with national postal museums, such as now exist in many countries, or with principal philatelic societies.

THE SPECIALIST'S VIEW

Artists' drawings are of many kinds, from the 'back of an envelope' type of preliminary sketch to the final artwork handed to the printer. The latter may with certain methods of printing be capable of being made directly into stamps; with others an intermediary in the person of a skilled engraver must interpret the design on a metal plate. This will be described in Chapter 5. Drawings vary in size from actual stamp size upwards, 4 (linear) times the finished stamp size being normal. Some designers prefer to work to actual stamp size, realizing that anything drawn to a magnified scale will suffer when it is reduced. With careful judgment, and the use of a reducing glass, it is however possible to avoid the temptation to include detail so fine that it becomes lost.

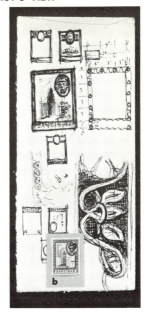

55a Zanzibar: artist's rough sketches for 1957 issue
  b Zanzibar: issued 1 shilling incorporating details from above sketches

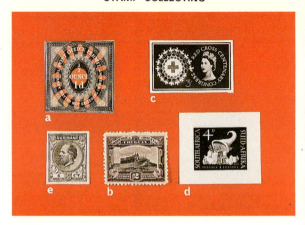

From artists' drawings the printer proceeds to produce **essays**. In collectors' parlance the term 'essay' is generally applied only to a design actually printed and then rejected (**a**, **b**), whereas strictly speaking all trial designs are essays at that stage including those actually used. Nor is it correct to apply the term to a mere illustration of an unadopted design (**c**, **d**), though these can give an equally fascinating glimpse of 'what might have been' and may well be all that is available to the collector making a study in depth of a particular issue.

A **proof** may well be a proof of an essay, or more likely a proof of an adopted design at an intermediate stage in the production of an issue (**e**). A die proof is a trial impression from a metal die, usually one that has been engraved by hand, and often at an

a   b   c

incomplete stage (**a**). Its purpose is to enable a judgment to be formed of the effectiveness of a design, of the clarity of its parts, and of its relative tone values. When a steel die has been completed to everyone's satisfaction it is hardened, so die proofs may be found labelled 'before' and 'after hardening'. Plate proofs are trials made (normally in black) from the finished printing plate, which contains as many impressions as there are to be stamps on the sheet. **Colour trials** may be virtually the same thing as plate proofs, except that they are more likely to be perforated so as to give a proper indication of the appearance of finished stamps; sometimes they are produced in great variety to enable the best possible selection to be made (**b**). A famous colour trial is the 2½d Prussian blue of the British 1935 Silver Jubilee issue, one or two sheets of which were confused with the brighter blue actually chosen, found their way to a post office, and were sold to the public. Some stamps of this nature are however no more than 'printer's waste', probably smuggled out illegally (**c**). A further category, 'prepared for use but not issued', means what it says, a frequent reason for cancellation being a sudden political change (**58a**).

When new stamps are ready for issue, examples are circulated (through the Universal Postal Union at Berne in Switzerland) to all other postal organizations so that they shall be recognizable as legitimate issues. Such stamps are usually marked with the word '**specimen**', either by overprinting or perforation (**b**, **c**). The equivalent word in other languages, such as *saggio* in Italian and *monster* in Dutch actually mean 'sample'. **Printers' samples**, in English terminology, are somewhat different; as the word implies, they are made by printers as advertisements of their workmanship, for circulation to prospective customers (**d**). Very often they closely resemble issued stamps but are in different colours and may have the printers' name overprinted on them (**59a**). So-called **black prints** are nothing more than reprints made for collectors (often with the aid of the original dies) (**59b**), and there are a number of other forms in which stamp-like prints are produced and legitimately sold to collectors – but not over post office counters, and so they are not valid for postage and not classed as postage stamps.

Whereas manufacturing **errors** in most things cause a reduction in value, those in stamps (unless they are design errors which affect every example until corrected) are greatly sought after – both for their rarity and, in many cases, the light they throw on methods of production. The famous 'Inverted Swan' of early Western Australia, for example, indicates that although the stamps were printed in one colour the printing plates were 'laid down' in two stages, the swans and the frame designs separately. Moreover a study of the wide margin of one specimen

showed a piece of the next stamp and proved it was not the swan that was inserted upside-down on the plate, but the frame.

More often inverted centres occur in two-coloured stamps through a whole sheet of paper being fed through the press the wrong way (**c**). If that is done with a single-coloured stamp it may result in nothing more spectacular than an inverted watermark. If one sheet is missed (perhaps through two sticking together) a 'missing centre' or 'missing colour' may be caused. A famous modern error of the Falkland Islands shows a 'wrong centre' – a ship intended for the $2\frac{1}{2}$d value appears on the 6d. There must have been a whole sheet printed, but only a dozen or so have been found.

Overprints and surcharges are a fruitful field for errors, particularly when set up in loose type by inexperienced printers (**a**, **b**). Inverted (**c**) and double (**d**) overprints and missing or wrong or interchanged letters or figures are the most frequent; also 'wrong fount' letters (picked in error or through shortage from amongst type of a different style or size), or even surcharges on the wrong basic stamp (**e**). It is by no means unknown for 'errors' of such kinds to be artificially manufactured either by underhand means or by irresponsible postal authorities seeking extra revenue from collectors – or to be 'rescued' from waste intended for destruction.

Conversely, there have been instances where genuine errors inadvertently released to the public have been deliberately reprinted in large quantities so as to prevent them from attaining an enhanced value (**61a**, **121a**).

Other kinds of error which may be encountered are a partial (**61b**) or complete lack of perforation, a defective watermark or even a completely wrong one, omission of phosphor lines, double printing (**61c**), printing on the gummed side of the paper, and various degrees of inaccurate registration between the colours of a design or between the design and its perforation. Quite amusing 'errors' are sometimes caused by paper becoming accidentally creased or folded in the course of printing.

A further class of error arises through one unit on a printing plate being made accidentally different from the others. As with the Western Australia Swan, part of the design may be misplaced, or the denomination may be wrong (resulting in one stamp appearing to be merely of the wrong colour when detached from the remainder) or the figures of value or some other part may be missing altogether, or the whole unit may be upside-down (resulting in *tête-bêche* pairs) or there may merely be some unspectacular dot or scratch which with some degree of imagination can be likened to a tear in the Queen's eye, an extra island on a map, or a stroke making an S into a $, or an F into an E (**d**).

Minor blemishes of this kind, if constant (that is, occurring on the corresponding stamp in every sheet) are called plate flaws. Those who see no significance in them call them 'flyspecks'. Those who study them (particularly on older stamps printed by lithography) can sometimes identify so many on a full sheet that they can actually locate every stamp's position on the sheet individually. This process is called **plating**. For all its fascination it is not only a very time-consuming task, but it also requires large quantities of suitable stamps and is not to be undertaken lightly.

The term **varieties**, often coupled with 'errors', is a vague one which may refer to minor errors, flyspecks and so forth, or alternatively to small variations in colour, perforation etc. from a basic stamp.

4. THE USES OF STAMPS

The first stamps were meant for clearly defined purposes within their own countries (**a**). They were simply receipts for payment of inland postage on letters up to certain weights. As time went on, things became more and more complicated; special-use categories were thought necessary by some postal organizations, while others were satisfied with a simple system. Ordinary stamps in everyday use for an indefinite period are called **definitives** (**b**).

Commemoratives are another very large group, issued to honour people (**c**) or to mark events (**d**) and anniversaries (**e**), and usually limited either in quantities printed or in their period of use. Occasionally, however, they continue in use long enough to become in effect definitives (**f**), and so a definite distinction cannot always be made.

Since World War II a quite separate category of **thematic** stamps (**g**) has come into being. These are pictorials neither printed in sufficient quantities to be called definitives, nor commemorating any particular event, but produced mainly to satisfy collectors – who in the last few decades have become increasingly interested in arranging their stamps according to subjects or themes rather than countries.

Provisionals are temporary issues, often hastily prepared and usually bearing surcharges or overprints – resulting from a change in government (**a**), currency (**b**) or postal rates (**c**), or from delays in the receipt of normal supplies from the printer (**d**).

Air stamps are of course intended for mail where the principal part of the journey is by air, but ordinary and air stamps tend to be used more or less indiscriminately. More certain distinguishing marks are either the blue post office labels inscribed *Par Avion* (**e**) (sometimes called 'vignettes') or the unofficial striped edge markings on air mail envelopes. In the pioneer years of air transport such mail often received handstamped 'cachets' bearing the air line's name or route, the weight of the letter, or other information. At that time, too, some countries produced quite long sets of air stamps (**f**) providing, in some cases, denominations for numerous rates and destinations; there were also many semi-official issues by both private and state-owned air lines – particularly in parts of South America where the mountainous terrain had discouraged road and rail development (**g**).

Express stamps (**c**) represent a special fee to cover the journey between the destination post office and the addressee – for which a special messenger may be required. Some such stamps (those of the USA for example) are inscribed 'Special Delivery' (**a**). One or two countries, such as Canada (**b**) and Colombia, have also issued air express stamps. Another variant is the **pneumatic post** system within certain cities of Italy, for which special stamps have been issued.

Registration, the system whereby valuable letters are signed for at every stage of their journey, has in some countries prompted special stamps to represent either the registration fee, or the fee and postage combined (**d**). The normal practice however is to use numbered labels bearing a letter R, coupled with sufficient ordinary postage stamps. The **Certified Mail** and **Acknowledgment of Receipt** services of the USA and Colombia (**f**) respectively are somewhat similar, and so are or were the **Insured Letter** schemes of Holland and Mexico (**e**); all have prompted special stamps.

   Parcels stamps (**a**, **b**) are a complex group because they
include those issued for use on state railways (**c**, **d**, **f**) – though
there is no very clear agreement amongst collectors as to
whether they are really postage stamps or (because of their
restricted area of use) 'locals'. (**Locals** are dealt with more fully
in Chapter 2.) The parcels stamps of Italy, which are sold at post
offices, are in double format and separated for use – one half
being attached to the packet and the other to a receipt (**e**).

   Newspaper stamps are sometimes merely the lowest
denomination of a series of ordinary stamps. The $\frac{1}{4}$d stamps of
Malta and other former British colonies, for example, were
primarily intended for local newspaper postage but they could

also be used in multiples and for making up larger amounts (**a**).
Several European countries have issued special stamps solely
for newspapers, including Belgian ones for parcels of papers
sent by train (**b**) and early Austrian affixed to the papers before
printing and cancelled by the newsprint itself. This category
can be extended to printed matter generally, also called 'second-
class' mail; here again a low denomination may be meant for
this purpose, or (as described in Chapter 3) stamps with one
phosphor line for the automatic segregation of such mail (**c**).
Pre-cancels are a curious anomaly. Used principally in France
and the USA (**d**, **e**), they are for bulk postings of commercial
printed matter. The cancelling of stamps before use (in fact by
the printers) would seem to be contrary to the object of
cancellation, which is the prevention of re-use, but this is largely
overcome by restricting their use to bulk mail, and latterly by
using different denominations from those for ordinary mail (**f**).

Postage Due stamps (**a**) are mainly a means of accounting for charges levied on unstamped or understamped letters. If postage has to be collected from recipients on delivery it defeats one of the main objects of the postage stamp, which is to simplify the process of actual payment for postal services at the start of a journey. In the early days of stamps there was some resistance to prepayment, particularly in Greece and Turkey where it amounted to an insult to suggest, by putting a stamp on a letter, that the addressee could not afford to pay! As a result the 19th century postage due issues of those countries were no less complex than the ordinary ones (**b**). Probably just as prevalent in Britain as in the Near East was the practice of sending unstamped envelopes which, when shown to the addressee with a demand for postage, were sufficient in themselves to convince him or her that the sender was still alive and well. British postage due stamps first appeared in 1914 and until recently the system was to collect double the deficiency by this method. The wording 'To Pay' now used (**c**) indicates that not only postage due is collected, but also customs duty, *poste restante* and other charges. The international sign of a large capital 'T' signifies 'Taxes' (in French), and in many cases stamps so overprinted (**d**) (or punched (**37e**)) have done duty as 'postage dues'.

Official stamps are used by government departments, not to prepay postage in the usual sense, but as a check on expenditure. For that reason some countries have even produced special stamps for different departments or ministries. Those of Argentina (**a**), Britain (**b**) and the USA (**c**) are the most frequently encountered, but the most curious emanated from South Australia (**d**) in the last century, with such overprints as 'C.D.' for 'Convict Department' and 'I.S.' for 'Inspector of Sheep'. Some official stamps bear the overprint 'O.S.' ('On Service') or its equivalent and some have these or other letters punched in them ('perfins' as described in Chapter 2). Nowadays, however, most governments use suitably marked postal stationery for official correspondence.

Frank stamps are somewhat similar, but are (or were) issued to private individuals or societies in some countries for free postage (**e**). **Military frank** stamps are issued free to servicemen (**f**, **g**).

Too late stamps are an uncommon kind (**a**). They represent a special fee payable for mail posted too late to catch the scheduled collection; in other words its initial sorting is speeded up rather than the final stage of its journey which might be 'special delivery.'

Charity stamps are a very large group consisting principally of stamps sold at a premium over their postal value – the difference being passed by the post office to a charitable organization. The best known are the children's charity or Pro Juventute ('for youth') series issued every autumn by Switzerland, which are used throughout the country as Christmas approaches (**b**). Eagerly bought because of their natural history, heraldic and similarly colourful designs, they enable the public as well as collectors to help worth-while causes. The one and only charity stamp issued by Britain was a resounding failure because of its dismal, uninspired design. In some countries not only have charity stamps appeared in excessive numbers, but also excessively high charity premiums have been imposed – a deterrent to collectors, let alone to genuine postal users (**c**).

Some charity stamps are, strictly speaking, **charity tax** stamps: the difference being that they pay no postage at all but represent a compulsory levy on all mail. They are particularly popular in the Near and Middle East where refugee and similar organizations are the beneficiaries (**a**, **b**). Many other 'worthy causes' can be found in Latin America, such as post office reconstruction (**c**), anti-tuberculosis (**d**) and earthquake relief funds. Tax stamps are considered to be collectable because their use is at times obligatory. The 'war tax' stamps issued in many British colonies during World War I merely represented additional postal charges necessitated by war conditions (**e**).

Telegraph stamps (**f**) (issued for prepayment of telegrams) had at one time a considerable following amongst collectors. This was largely because postage stamps were very frequently used on telegraph forms and when special issues appeared they usually bore a close resemblance. Postage stamps, especially the higher denominations, are worth less with telegraphic cancellations when these are distinguishable (for example those

of India (**a**)), but in cases where they cannot for certain be told apart, stamps with telegraphic obliterations are often considered more desirable because they are neater (**b**).

Fiscal or **Revenue** stamps are similarly less collected now than at one time. To the specialist their chief interest probably lies in their resemblances to postage stamps, the same printers and methods of production being very often used and the designs being often similar (**c**). As with the telegraph service, postage stamps have frequently 'doubled' as fiscals, and this accounts for the inscription 'Postage and Revenue' on many British and Commonwealth stamps (**d**), as well as the very high denominations found in some issues – amounts which could not possibly have been needed for postage.

Unlike telegraphic cancellations, revenue markings can almost always be distinguished, being usually by rubber stamp (**e**) but often by pen and ink (**f**), and they cause a drastic reduction in value. They indicate use on business receipts, licences of many kinds, tax documents, contracts, passports and the like. Sometimes stamps intended as fiscals have been allowed, officially or otherwise, for postal use; they are known as **postal fiscals** (**g**).

Stamps used by the **United Nations** organization and its agencies comprise a special class. They are in a sense Official stamps without a country, though they are mostly associated with Switzerland and the USA (**a**) and some with Austria and Canada. Between the World Wars there were issues for the League of Nations (**b**) and International Labour Office, over-printed on those of Switzerland. After the establishment of the United Nations, similar stamps were produced both for the main offices in Geneva, New York and Vienna and for numerous subsidiary offices such as the World Meteorological Organiza-tion (**c**) and the International Telecommunications Union.

The **Universal Postal Union**, itself set up in 1874, came much later under the wing of the UN and has its own stamps too (**d**). This is the international organization to which the post offices of all countries belong, and which regulates all matters concerning international mail – such as limits of weight and cost and methods of charging for understamped letters. It also has certain jurisdiction over stamps (requiring for example the value to be expressed in Arabic figures) and at one time stipulated the green/red/blue UPU colour scheme for stamps intended for overseas printed matter, postcards and letters

respectively (**a**, **b**, **c**). It holds a congress every four years, which is usually the subject of a commemorative issue by the host country (**143e**).

A number of other limited postal unions and formal agreements allow mail to pass at less than the 'overseas' rate. One such exists between Spain and the former Spanish parts of Latin America (**e**); another applies reciprocally between Britain and Ireland.

Before the UPU came into being and mail routes became fully organized, and before many smaller states issued their own stamps, some European countries maintained post offices overseas. In most instances these merely used the stamps of the parent organization, which can then be distinguished by their postmarks (**d**) and are best collected on cover. 19th-century British stamps are quite often found with postmarks of Malta (**f**) and Gibraltar; less frequently with those of a host of other places like Valparaiso in Chile, Kingston in Jamaica and Alexandria in Egypt.

Similarly French may be found used in South America (**above**), Turkey, individual French colonies, and many other places. Italy, Germany, Russia and others had overseas offices too, mostly in association with their consulates in seaports. The system continued well into the present century, particularly in Morocco and Arabia, mainly using stamps overprinted and surcharged with local currency. Much in demand are stamps used in smaller territories before they had their own issues (**168c**), such as Indian used in Aden (**75a**) and Austrian in Liechtenstein.

Other types of mail also give rise to stamps 'used abroad'. One is the **paquebot** system whereby mail posted on board ship is cancelled on arrival at the next port. Thus it is possible to find British stamps postmarked at French ports (**75b**) or South African at British; in addition the word 'Paquebot' is often handstamped on the envelope. Another kind arises from double 'reply-paid' cards, to both halves of which the sender affixes stamps of his own country, so that the reply half in due course receives a 'foreign' postmark on its return journey (**75c**); this sort of cancellation however usually has no particular story to tell about postal routes and methods. Less interesting still are

stamps that have collected 'foreign' postmarks through being re-directed or through having missed the canceller at the start of their journey; these are no more than freaks.

The term **Interprovincials** usually refers to stamps of Australian and South African states (former British colonies) used in other states of the unified countries before or even after the first general series were issued (**d**). There are many other instances of stamps being valid within a larger territory than is indicated on them – for example those of individual Malayan states throughout Malaysia, those of the Australian Antarctic Territory in Australia itself, and British 'regionals' throughout the UK (**e**). Stamps so used are however thought of as little more than curiosities and must be considered worth less than stamps used in their correct location.

5. HOW STAMPS ARE PRINTED

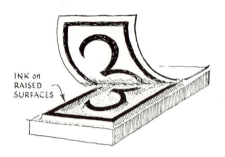

INK on RAISED SURFACES

Nowadays when stamps are needed by the million, and are frequently multi-coloured, the machinery for printing them is extremely complex. Nevertheless, the principles have changed very little since the days of the first stamps, nor do they differ in most respects from those of other classes of printing; so there is no difficulty in recognizing and understanding the basic methods.

There are three main processes, differing in the manner in which the design appears on the surface of the printing plate; it may be raised, sunk or flat and these three will be considered in that order.

The simplest of all is the **letterpress** process, everyday examples and variants of which include newspapers, train tickets, the rubber stamp on an office desk, and even the postmark on a letter. In every case the type or the plate has its printing surface raised above those parts which are not to print. When ink is applied with a pad or roller it adheres to these raised surfaces, from which it is then transferred to the paper under slight pressure.

HOW STAMPS ARE PRINTED

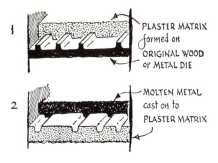

1 — PLASTER MATRIX *formed on* ORIGINAL WOOD or METAL DIE

2 — MOLTEN METAL *cast on to* PLASTER MATRIX

The wood-cut, which in the mid-19th century was a standard method of illustrating books (and had by then been brought to an astonishing degree of perfection), is another example of letterpress. Even in the 18th century such blocks could be stereotyped – that is, reproductions could be made in an alloy metal by means of an intermediate mould of plaster of Paris or similar substance. In 1841 electrotyping was invented. It entailed making an impression in wax, lead or other material which, after being coated with blacklead, could receive a layer of copper by electrolytic action; this copper shell could then be removed and backed with a solid soft alloy metal and faced with steel, nickel or other hard coating.

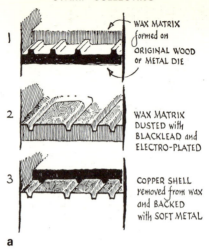

1 — WAX MATRIX *formed on* ORIGINAL WOOD or METAL DIE

2 — WAX MATRIX DUSTED with BLACKLEAD and ELECTRO-PLATED

3 — COPPER SHELL *removed from* wax and BACKED with SOFT METAL

a

It is easy to see how, by means of either process, a printing plate can be built up capable of printing, say, 100 or 200 stamps simultaneously from a single original die. It may be done in two stages; for example a stereotype may be made in a multiple of 10 which can then itself be stereotyped 10 times to form a plate of 100 units.

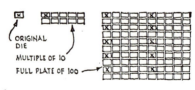

ORIGINAL DIE
MULTIPLE OF 10
FULL PLATE OF 100

b

The preparation of the original die calls for craftsmanship of the highest order; a very rare skill is needed to cut a design accurately into a hard substance (from wood to steel) when it is the tiny breadth of material left between the hollows which determines the thickness of every printed line, but to be able to do so within the square inch or so which represents a stamp is little short of miraculous. True, border patterns and regular lines of shading can be produced mechanically, but only a master engraver can produce a lifelike portrait (**a, b**). This kind of engraving is called *en épargne*, and two of its greatest exponents in the realm of stamps have been Joubert de la Ferté, engraver of Queen Victoria's head for de la Rue in 1855 (**c**), and Eugène Mouchon, who produced several European masterpieces (**d, e**). The delicacy of such work became impracticable to reproduce as printing became faster and more mechanized. Nowadays letterpress 'line' blocks are almost always produced photomechanically (**f, g**), and thus completely lack the rare touch of the artist-craftsman; the process is however hardly used for stamps any more.

79

80 Norway: 15 øre definitive, typographed, 1908

81 Norway: 15 øre definitive, recess-printed, 1962

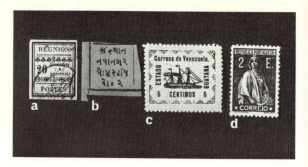

Letterpress is also correctly known as surface-printing. Unfortunately collectors have long used the term **typography** which to printers means only the art and practice of printing from type (as in books and other printed matter). This less exact word will be found (usually abbreviated to 'typo' for 'typographed') in practically every catalogue and other book on stamps.

Overprints and surcharges are often set up from printers' type, especially those produced in an emergency. Even a few actual stamps, of a primitive or provisional nature, have been printed in this way; these are referred to as **type-set** (**a, b, c**).

The characteristics of a stamp printed by 'typography' are: firstly the slight relief effect (often visible on the back and, in the case of an unused stamp, through the gum) caused by the pressure of the lines of the design on the paper; and secondly the tendency of the ink to be squeezed outwards from the edges of each line or coloured area, making what should be clean-cut edges into darker, slightly blotchy ones when seen through a magnifier. Generally, too, the overall appearance of such stamps is coarse compared with those produced by other processes (**d**).

Letterpress plates are prone to damage by accidental cuts and scratches which show as white (uninked) marks on the actual stamp. These are sometimes significant enough to be collectable, as mentioned at the end of Chapter 3.

HOW STAMPS ARE PRINTED

INK STAYS
ONLY IN
RECESSES WHEN
PLATE IS WIPED

Next is **recess-printing**. If lines are scratched on a smooth metal plate, ink is wiped across them, and the surface is then wiped clean, a little ink will stay in the scratches. Now if soft or damp paper is pressed hard against the plate, it will pick up ink from the scratches and take an impression in reverse which stands up from the surface in tiny ridges. This process was known as early as the 15th century, and used by artists as illustrious as Dürer, Rembrandt and Rubens. It is also called intaglio and sometimes line-engraving.

Only in 1800 did copper plates begin to give way to steel, with the result that many more impressions could be made before they became seriously worn. Book illustrations from steel engravings are familiar; they were superior in many ways to wood engravings but had the disadvantage of having to be printed separately from the text and bound in afterwards. Just before the time of the first stamps, Jacob Perkins had perfected a method whereby an engraved steel die could be hardened. By means of great pressure a reversed impression could then be made on to a soft steel cylinder, known as a transfer roller. This in its turn could be hardened and, again under pressure, rocked on to a soft steel plate as many times as there were to be stamps in a sheet. These final versions, being again reversed, resembled the original die and were themselves hardened before being printed from.

DESIGN IN RELIEF ON PERIMETER OF ROLLER

HARDENED STEEL TRANSFER ROLLER FIRMLY HELD IN BEARINGS OF PRESS AND FREE TO REVOLVE

POLISHED SOFTENED STEEL PLATE

The nature of the line-engraving process was considered by the British authorities of 1840 to be a powerful, if only partial, protection against forgers. Perkins, however, had also invented an 'engine' which would engrave elaborate mechanical patterns directly on to steel, patterns of such delicacy and variety that once the setting of the machine had been disturbed it was impossible ever to repeat them. That of course was ideal both for stamps and for banknotes. Further, apart from the highly skilled operation of cutting the original die, partly by hand and partly by machine, it was also possible to engrave on to the transfer roller (or on to another reversed plate) so that on the finished stamp a line originally cut in recess might appear white on a coloured background.

Other mechanical, chemical and photographic means of engraving have been devised, but the printer by recess still relies essentially on the master die painstakingly cut by the artist with his burin. Amongst the greatest names in the past were Charles and Frederick Heath, engravers of Queen Victoria's head on the Penny Black, and William Humphrys who copied it fifteen years later and engraved many 'classics' (**a**). At the present day the best known is probably Czeslaw Slania, whose work has been used by many printers for an even greater number of countries (**b, 145b**).

The characteristic of a recess-printed stamp is the fact that the lines of its design stand up above the surface of the paper. Usually this is true to such an extent that a 'rubbing' taken with silver paper produces a clear impression of the design. The apparent colour can vary greatly according to the actual depth of lines of shading, as well as their distance apart (**c**).

Weak entries from the transfer roller on to the printing plate often give rise to hand-retouching which can be detected on the finished stamp. Misplaced ones insufficiently burnished out give rise to **re-entries**, which are doublings of the whole or part of a design.

GREASY INK
ADHERES ONLY
TO PARTS OF
PLATE PREVIOUSLY
INKED

Photogravure, the modern development of recess-printing, will be dealt with later. **Lithography**, or flat printing, deserves to come first for it is far older.

The principle of lithography is the mutual repulsion of oil and water. Originally a flat polished limestone plate was used (hence the name, from the Greek *lithos*, stone). A design is drawn on the stone in greasy ink, which adheres to it. If the whole stone is now wetted, the inked part will be unaffected, but the rest will absorb water. If next the whole surface is inked, the wet part will be unreceptive but the parts originally inked will accept more ink. Thus a piece of paper pressed on the plate will take up an impression of the original design.

Instead of the design being drawn directly on to the stone, it can be on special paper from which, by means of a press, it is transferred to the plate. Such 'transfers' can be prepared from originals produced by another process, or they may be themselves lithographed (this explains certain issues of stamps which exist by two different printing methods only distinguishable on close examination). With their aid a complete printing plate can be built up. The procedure for producing a multiple transfer, which is itself reproduced repeatedly until a plate of sufficient size has been constructed, is similar to that of multiplying a letterpress or recess die, but has the great advantage of not involving molten metal or heavy pressures.

Those are the basic principles of lithography. Zinc or aluminium plates are now used instead of stone, and photographic

HOW STAMPS ARE PRINTED

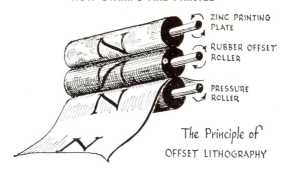

ZINC PRINTING PLATE

RUBBER OFFSET ROLLER

PRESSURE ROLLER

The Principle of OFFSET LITHOGRAPHY

reproductions can now be transferred to them by several different methods. Refinements in the manner of preparing and inking the plates have brought the process to an impressive degree of perfection, but until the introduction of the offset press it was only possible to obtain satisfactory prints on a very smooth paper. In this type of machine the inked design is impressed by the hard plate not directly on to the paper but on to a revolving rubber roller from which it is then transferred to the paper. Any slight unevenness of the paper is thus countered by the resilience of the rubber, and a regular matt print is obtained.

The characteristics of a lithographed stamp are primarily its flat appearance – the lines of the design being neither raised above the surface nor impressed into it – and the evenness of the colour of large and small areas. They are however prone to repetitive flaws caused during the process of building up a plate by blemishes either in the original, or in the transfer, or in the final plate. Also the offset process can cause accidental doubling of a design.

88 Crete: postage due 1 lepton, lithographed 1901

89 Norway: 15 øre definitive, photogravure, 1952

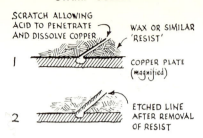

Photogravure has been left to be described quite separately, not because it is any harder to understand, but because it is really only a special kind of recess-printing.

It is well known that copper plates can be etched with acid, instead of being mechanically engraved with a burin. If a thin layer of wax or other acid-resisting substance (called a 'resist') is applied and then scratched with a design, the acid will only eat away the copper where the scratch has exposed it. This is how innumerable artists have produced etchings, from which prints can be made in exactly the same way as from true engravings.

Now if a photographic print of a picture or design is made on special sensitized paper coated with coloured gelatine (called a carbon tissue) and then pressed on a plate of polished copper previously dusted with powdered resin, a simple washing in water will disolve the paper and all the gelatine *except* that hardened by the action of light. The effect is just the same as before: when treated with acid the copper will only be eaten away in those parts which are unprotected by hard gelatine.

HOW STAMPS ARE PRINTED

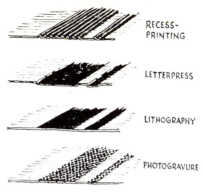

RECESS-
PRINTING

LETTERPRESS

LITHOGRAPHY

PHOTOGRAVURE

91 characteristics of the four processes (much magnified)

In practice much better results are obtained if, in addition to the design, a tiny grid of ruled squares (about six to the millimetre) is photographed also on to the carbon tissue. This splits the design up into tiny dots, each of which becomes a minute recess on the printing plate. In the highlights of the design these recesses dwindle to nothing, and in the deep tones they become the same size as the spaces of the squared grid, and thus hold enough ink to give an effect of solid colour.

After being etched, the printing surface (which is usually in the form of a cylinder) is hardened, usually by chromium plating.

Repetition of an original design to build up the carbon tissue for the plate for a complete sheet of stamps is carried out photographically by a special camera incorporating a 'step-and-repeat' mechanism

With the exception of certain issues of South Africa (**a**), photogravure stamps can be recognized by the 'screen' of tiny dots of which their design is composed, though (unlike the rather similar 'half-tone' of newspaper illustrations) these are usually invisible to the naked eye. More important is the fact that colour tones are infinitely variable from dark to light (**b**), and can thus exactly reproduce what the artist draws on paper with brush or spray ('air brush'). They are often produced on fast-running rotary presses, necessitating quick-drying inks and soft-surfaced paper, and are thus comparatively easily damaged by abrasion or chemical action (**c**).

Later developments of lithography, it should be remembered, can produce a very similar 'screened' appearance, but the individual dots are usually sharper and the general effect flatter (**d**); areas of solid colour (**e, f**) completely lack the rich texture associated with photogravure.

Multi-colour printing is not new to stamps; in fact some of the trial designs produced before the Penny Black (**56a**) were in more than one colour. Its principal difficulty is the accurate registration of colours to each other on so minute a scale, especially since paper is a flexible material and very susceptible to changes in humidity. This is a particular problem in recess-printing; the Giori type of press, in which several colours are printed at one operation, overcomes it ingeniously by a special method of inking and wiping a single plate (**a**). Most of the difficulties have also been solved in modern photogravure (**b**) and lithographic presses, though it is well known that errors occasionally occur in which one or more colours fail to print.

Sometimes two processes are used on a single stamp – particularly photogravure (**c**) or lithography (**d**) combined with ordinary recess-printing. This produces a combination of soft colouring and sharp definition suited to many kinds of design.

Another process, **embossing**, is occasionally used, very rarely on its own and usually combined with letterpress (**a**) or less frequently with recess-printing (**b**) or photogravure. It is done with a reversed relief die like those used for coinage, which forces the paper against a 'matrix' of plaster, metal or other substance, and is more familiar on postal stationery than on adhesive stamps (**c**).

When a metallic appearance is required it is usually achieved with metallic inks, but a modern alternative consists of very thin metallic foil which is applied from a ribbon under pressure – rather on the same principle as a typewriter (**e**). There are also stamps printed and embossed on metal foil which is backed (in order to preserve the form of the embossing) by papier mâché or similar solid material of substantial thickness and then individually cut to shape (**d**).

An embossed effect of a different kind can be produced by a process using plastic 'inks' which by means of heat are solidified from powders in a similar way to the operation of modern electrostatic document-copying machines (**a**).

Several other printing methods have a curiosity value. They include direct photography (siege stamps of Mafeking), type-writing (early Uganda) and rubber-stamping by hand (New Republic of South Africa (**b**)). But a search through any collection will reveal interesting variations on the standard methods. No two printers in fact use precisely the same methods even for the same basic process, and their individual characteristics are a fruitful field of study for the specialist collector.

6. WAYS TO COLLECT

Almost everyone's inclination, on beginning to collect stamps, is to keep everything that comes along, regardless of date or country. That is no bad thing, for it enables a broad view to be taken over the entire range. Later on, a more restricted field may be chosen; not only can this be done with far greater confidence with the advantage of a general knowledge of all the options available, but also that same general knowledge, once acquired, will be useful as a background in studies and contacts of all kinds – in just the same way as the specialist in art or architecture of a particular period or country should never be blinkered to his neighbour's interests.

General collecting was at one time almost universal. Everyone set out with the vague ambition of acquiring a copy of every stamp ever issued, undeterred by the fact that of some rarities only a very few existed at all. Printed albums were produced which provided spaces for every one. Even when the futility of it was realized, many people continued to be general collectors partly because of the sheer fascination of all stamps and partly because occasional changes in their interests (or changes in potential sources of supply) meant that to whatever subjects or countries those interests turned they would already have a nucleus on which to build. The coming of loose-leaf albums meant that a general collection could be trimmed to suit the purse and yet still look attractive. If only a set to the value of a shilling could be afforded, one could turn a blind eye to the higher values up to, perhaps, a pound, and not even leave spaces for them. Financial gain apart, to many collectors there is more enjoyment in collecting a dozen 'short' sets than one 'full' one for the same expenditure.

The first break with general collecting is a decision to confine one's interests to a single group. British collectors have long tended to concentrate on the one-time British Empire and to discard everything 'foreign'. This particular tradition still survives in the Gibbons Part I catalogue which continues to list all the

issues of those same countries (**a, b, c, d**) – including even some which long ago left what is now the Commonwealth, such as Ireland and South Africa. Collectors in France, Germany, Italy etc. tended to concentrate (and still do) on their own groups or spheres of influence, or on the stamps of Western Europe as a whole (**e, f, g, h**). There is a natural tendency to be interested in the issues of one's own country, but on the other hand a reaction against that may lead to unexpected pleasures amongst the obscurer stamps of some quite remote country. True, these will be far harder to find than the 'run-of-the-mill' popular issues, but on the other hand, once found they will be a good deal cheaper relative to their scarcity (**i, j, k, l**).

STAMP COLLECTING

Collecting habits are constantly changing – under all sorts of pressures, but mainly because of the sheer numbers of new stamps constantly being produced by every one of the 240 or so issuing authorities in the world.

The pleasures of the hunt and the satisfaction of the 'kill' are often greater than the ultimate satisfaction of possession. Once a set or a series is complete it is possible that there is no more to be said or done; it is either put away and forgotten, or disposed of so that a fresh start may be made on something else. With stamps however that is not by any means always the case, for there is always the possibility of looking at them in a new light, a fresh context. A 'straight' used set may be discovered to be a fruitful start for a new study of out-of-the-way cancellations or to provide evidence of the dates of use of certain shades or perforations; a mint set may provide the nucleus for a 'thematic' or subject collection of birds or landscapes or portraits, or by means of adding blocks and strips it may be greatly expanded into a 'plating' study (see Chapter 3).

Many people have more than one collection: perhaps a serious one and a 'sideline' one, perhaps a semi-general one covering a group of countries and a specialized one treating a single issue or even a single stamp in great detail. To specialize to the extent of only collecting variations of one issue, or even of one stamp, obviously means a measure of devotion to the hobby that not everyone possesses, or indeed would want to possess. Apart from time, patience and skills of certain kinds in considerable quantity, it may demand a considerable knowledge of some of a great variety of other subjects: geography, commerce, social and political history, chemistry, printing techniques and so forth.

Postal history has been touched on in Chapter 2. Innumerable forms can be taken by a collection on these lines, and at the outset it is not likely to be possible to foresee in which direction it will grow. That will often be dictated by the amount of material actually available, and its cost. If too large a group (for example 'Germany' or 'China') is chosen the scope may after a while have to be narrowed to a single facet such as one state, one postal route or one historical period.

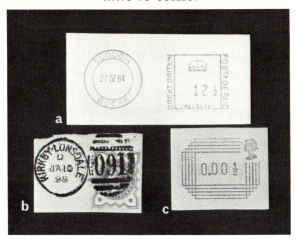

If **postmarks** alone are studied there is an equal danger of biting off more than one can chew. One fascinating sideline, for those so inclined, is the collecting of the numeral 'killer' cancellations used by many countries in the 19th century – each town and village having its own number, usually in an alphabetical sequence (**b**). Like much else in this hobby, however, the result may appear deadly dull to others – even to fellow collectors!

Postmarks are not confined to the actual cancellations on stamps. They include all kinds of other markings on letters – arrival marks, 'missent' marks, indications of postage due, weights, routes and methods of transport – the list is endless. There is also a wealth of markings to be seen and studied on pre-stamp letters (**17**). Even **meter** marks (**a**), the almost universal substitute for stamps, have their devotees, and this particular field has been expanded in recent years to include 'stamps' printed by publicly accessible coin-operated machines (**c**).

The growth of **thematic** collecting was an inevitable consequence of the proliferation of new issues. Unfortunately there has been a kind of rebound in that this growth has itself encouraged an even greater number of new issues designed to appeal to collectors of every popular subject but in fact only causing despair by making the goal of completion recede ever faster. Subjects that have been 'done to death' include, for example, the Olympic Games (**a**) and Space (**b**); the sheer quantity and high face value of such issues put out by countries and agencies of indifferent repute are sufficient to deter the keenest collector – whose incentive is still further reduced when he finds that as a result his own stamps are losing their actual value.

However, plenty of themes exist which have not suffered in this way – cats for example, or airships or armour; thousands could be found. Some collectors find amusement in entirely different directions: design errors on stamps, or stamps only printed in black, or stamps showing in their face values a series of numbers from 1 onwards (**c**) (not easy when it comes to numbers like 79).

The mounting and display of a thematic collection is a large part of its pleasure, and will be a mirror of one's own tastes, knowledge, skill, and perhaps sense of humour. 'Paintings on

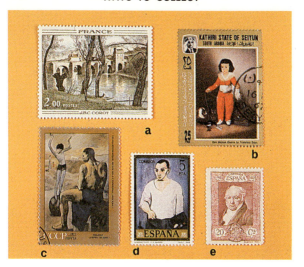

stamps' (**a**, **b**, **c**, **29**), for example could be classified under artists and could include, where they exist, portraits of the artists on stamps (**d**, **e**); there could be general headings of periods or nationalities and 'schools'. Or, alternatively, the pictures could be classified under the galleries where they are to be found. Or again they could be arranged according to subject matter. Loose-leaf album pages would be used and the 'writing up' could include as much or as little as one feels inclined or able. Some collectors would, for instance, try to obtain a postcard or similar reproduction of each painting and mount it alongside the stamp. So similarly with any other subject. Many subjects can be well explained and displayed with the aid of maps. There is a danger that the stamps themselves may become submerged in all kinds of extraneous matter, but if that kind of arrangement gives pleasure to the owner and instructs or amuses others its main objects are fulfilled.

102 stamp catalogues covering various groups of foreign countries

The question of 'showing' at stamp exhibitions will not be covered in this book. As with other specialized shows, their conduct and the rules laid down for and by judges are not always acceptable or even comprehensible to the uninitiated (particularly in relation to thematic exhibits). That is not to say that a great deal cannot be learnt from attending exhibitions, but the conditions of actual participation may seem to defeat the pleasure of getting a collection together.

Stamp **catalogues** have been published ever since collecting began to be taken seriously. Like collections themselves, they have changed character over the years, and general catalogues covering the entire world have given way to sectionalized ones. Gibbons' Part I ('British Commonwealth') has already been mentioned. Gibbons' 'foreign' catalogues have gradually been more and more subdivided over the years, and at the time of writing are in what may be thought a somewhat confused form,

103 catalogues covering various specialised groups and subjects

partly geographical, partly alphabetical and partly following the former colonial or postal spheres of influence. This means that countries like the Philippines and Togo are fragmented, and even countries which one might expect to find together like Algeria and Tunisia are in different volumes. If one turns to continental publishers one finds similarly frustrating illogicalities.

With this constant expansion of general catalogues come two divergent tendencies: on the one hand the development of the 'simplified' catalogue, which ignores watermarks and perforations and all but the most obvious variations from the basic stamp, and on the other the 'specialized' catalogue which goes to the opposite extreme by listing and pricing every possible known variation. In recent years even the simplified catalogue has burst its bounds and been split, encyclopedia-like, into more than one book; its main function is to give the general and the thematic collector an overall view of what exists. For the thematic enthusiasts, however, yet another kind is growing up: the check-lists based on single subjects. Though these take away much of the pleasure of the search, they do save the expense of buying catalogues of the whole world's stamps merely for the sake of those which happen to portray birds or space rockets or whatever is of interest.

Sudan 1948

1948 (1 Jan). OFFICIAL. Nos. 96/102 optd with Type O 3, and 103/111 with Type O 4.

023 22	1 m. black and orange	5	5
024	2 m. orange and chocolate	5	5
025	3 m. mauve and green	5	5
026	4 m. deep-green and chocolate	5	5
027	5 m. olive-brown and black	5	5
028	10 m. rose-red and black	8	8
029	15 m. ultramarine and chestnut	8	8
030 23	2 p. purple and orange-yellow	8	8
031	3 p. red-brown and deep blue	12	8
032	4 p. ultramarine and black	30	12
	a. Perf 13		
033	5 p. brown-orange and deep green	40	30
034	6 p. greenish blue and black	45	30
035	8 p. bluish green and black	55	35
036	10 p. black and mauve	85	60
037	20 p. pale blue and deep blue	2·50	1·10
038	50 p. carmine and ultramarine	6·00	4·00
023/38	Set of 16	10·00	6·50

120	4½ p. black and ultramarine	1·25	1·50
	a. Black and steel blue	1·25	1·50
121	6 p. black and carmine	85	60
122	20 p. black and purple	2·75	2·75
115/122	Set of 8	7·00	7·00

Designs:—2½ p. Kassala Jebel; 3 p. Sagia (water wheel); 3½ p. Port Sudan; 4 p. Gordon Memorial College; 4½ p. Nile Post Boat; 6 p. Suakin; 20 p. GPO, Khartoum.

1950 (1 July). OFFICIAL AIR. Nos 115/22 optd with Type O 4.

039	2 p. black and blue-green (R.)	90	90
040 27	2 p. light blue and red-orange	1·00	1·00
041	3 p. reddish purple and blue	1·00	70
042	3½ p. purple-brown and yellow-brown	1·25	1·75
043	4 p. brown and light blue	1·25	1·50
044	4½ p. black and ultramarine (R.)	2·00	3·75
	a. Black and steel blue	2·00	3·75
045	6 p. black and carmine (R.)	1·50	2·00
046	20 p. black and purple (R.)	6·00	9·50
039/46	Set of 8	13·00	19·00

34 Ibex   **35** Cotton Picking

(Des Col. W. L. Atkinson (1 m., 2 m., 4 m., 5 m., 10 m., 3 p., 3½ p., 20 p.), Col. E. A. Stanton (50 p.), others from photographs. Typo.)

1951 (1 Sept). T 34/5 and similar designs. Chalk-surfaced paper. W 7. P 14 (millième values) or 13 (piastre values).

123	1 m. black and orange	5	5
124	2 m. black and bright blue	5	5
125	3 m. black and green	20	40
126	4 m. black and yellow-green	5	5
127	5 m. black and purple (shades)	5	5
128	10 m. black and pale blue	8	5
129	15 m. black and chestnut (shades)	10	5
130	2 p. deep blue and pale blue (shades)	25	8
131	3 p. brown and ultramarine	25	8
	a. Brown and deep blue	25	10
132	3½ p. bright arn & red-brn (shades)	25	10

2 Gunboat Zafir   24

1944 (1 Jan). POSTAGE DUE. Arabic inscriptions at foot altered. Chalk-surfaced paper. Typo. W 7. P 14.

D1 D2	2 m. black and brown-orange	55	80
D..	4 m. brown and green	80	2·00
D..	10 m. green and mauve	1·00	1·25
D..	20 m. ultramarine and carmine	2·50	4·25

104 part of the listing of Sudan in Gibbons' catalogue

Stamp catalogues have always been arranged in a fairly standard way, with most of the information tabulated in columns. Each stamp is identified by a serial number, followed by a 'type' number referring to an illustration, then the face value or denomination and the colour or colours. Usually there are two columns of prices, the first being always for unused specimens and the second for used. Sometimes there are other columns giving information such as the value 'on cover' or of pairs or blocks, and if so they are clearly explained. So far as possible the stamps are grouped in 'sets' in the way that they are likely to be collected, though opinions often differ on what constitutes a set.

Catalogues do indeed differ a good deal from one another, and it is unfortunate and confusing that no agreement has ever been reached between publishers in different countries on the basic serial numbering of stamps. The best that has been achieved is that some specialized single-country catalogues

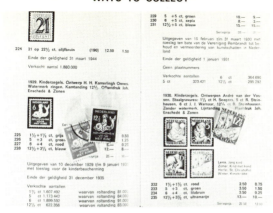

105 part of the listing of Netherlands stamps in a specialised catalogue

quote against each stamp the numbers of Gibbons, Yvert (France), Scott (USA) etc. Continental collections and dealers almost invariably use Yvert numbers. The worth of a catalogue can be judged from the amount of information it provides. It ought to describe stamp designs accurately and to name the designer and/or source of the picture. It ought to give the printing process and the printer's and engraver's names. It ought to describe the perforation and watermark, as well as anything unusual about the paper. It ought to name the colour, possibly in relation to a known standard. It ought to give the date of issue (or if that is not known, the earliest known date of use) and if there is a range of shades it should indicate the period of use of each. It ought to warn of the existence of forgeries, reprints and similar 'traps' and to give some help towards identifying them. It should also contain enough cross-references to assist identification – for example, to warn about a subsequent similar series with perhaps a different watermark. Specialized catalogues may give additional information such as the quantities printed and sold, the numbers of printing plates, and the existence and value of essays, proofs, commemorative covers, collectors' packs and similar material.

106 part of the first page of the Austria listing in Gibbons' catalogue

Following the basic listing of a stamp there will be found listed any 'varieties' that exist – such as major printing defects and errors, different phosphor markings, or variations in perforation from the main listing. The method of listing has to suit the circumstances; if almost an entire series exists in several different gauges of perforation a tabulated arrangement of price columns may be adopted, with a '†' or similar symbol to indicate any combination which does not exist. Varieties of doubtful authenticity (such as those produced by connivance within the printing works, or otherwise sold illicitly) are excluded but should be mentioned in footnotes.

With the development of multi-colour lithography, coloured illustrations have become common in the smaller, one-country catalogues. Whether coloured or black they are usually reduced in size to save space ($\frac{3}{4}$ linear is normal) though overprints and surcharges are normally full-size to facilitate checking for variations and forgeries. Enlargements of parts of stamps are

107 part of a dealer's price list

sometimes provided too, so as to explain minor points of difference between printings.

A catalogue is primarily a dealer's price list, and it is rare to find one without prices at all, though some are compiled on the principle of 'fair' or 'average' valuations, either by an association of dealers or by someone in touch with the trade but independent of it. The pricing always refers to selling, not buying, and for other purposes can never be more than an approximate guide (see Chapter 7), but that and the constant need to add new issues mean that catalogues quickly become out of date. The expense of buying a new edition whenever one is published is beyond many collectors, and in spite of the introduction of computer-based type-setting (for which this kind of book is especially suited) publishers are powerless to resist rising costs, and inevitably the law of diminishing returns forces higher and higher the prices of these essential aids to collecting.

Conversely there are very adequate price lists available at nominal cost, or even free, from many dealers, and one of them in conjunction with an out-of-date catalogue will provide a realistic enough picture for many purposes.

The idea of loose-leaf catalogues has often been mooted, but the vast number of changes (editorial as well as pricing) inevitable in every edition makes it impracticable.

108 selections of a) beginner's albums and guides, b) loose-leaf albums and c) cover albums

109 various types of stock book

Loose-leaf albums are of course commonplace and used by most collectors who have passed the 'schoolboy' stage. Albums can broadly be divided into three types: the fixed-leaf kind with a nominal allocation of space to each country, the loose-leaf kind with totally blank pages giving complete freedom, and the printed leaf kind which provides a ruled and often illustrated space for every stamp according to the catalogue list. At one time it was perfectly possible to produce this third kind for all the world in one volume; later on, a division into two or three, as with catalogues, was still practicable. Nowadays there is something of a revival of similar albums, but confined to stamps of one country only, and loose-leaved so that extra pages can be added for new issues. Some are of the 'hingeless' kind, with transparent pockets into which the stamps can be harmlessly slipped.

Special albums are made to house covers, postcards, etc., which if mounted in any quantity inside an ordinary binder will bulge it unduly. They usually comprise transparent pockets, so allowing both sides to be seen if desired. The page size of albums generally is tending to increase, so as to cope with bigger stamps, longer sets, se-tenant blocks, miniature sheets and the like. It is now difficult to obtain the miniature kind which used to be popular for 'sideline' collections.

Stock books provide a half-way house between the unsorted accumulation and the finally arranged album. They consist of card leaves with transparent strips into which stamps can be slipped loosely, and are useful for storing duplicates.

a MOUNT CLOSE TO (BUT CLEAR OF) TOP OF STAMP & LIGHTLY MOISTENED AT EACH END

UNDERSIDE OF STAMP (NOTE THAT IT CAN BE TURNED RIGHT BACK FOR EXAMINATION) ALBUM LEAF

b CLEAR ACETATE

CLEAR OR BLACK ACETATE GUMMED ON UNDERSIDE

ALBUM LEAF

HOW TO USE HINGES & HINGELESS MOUNTS

EDGE OF STAMP GRIPPED BY SEAM BETWEEN LAYERS

Early collectors were content to paste stamps into their books. Quantities of stamps were also stuck decoratively on to firescreens, tables and walls. If the sticking did not ruin them, the attempts to extricate them did. Unused stamps could be stuck with their own gum. Later the advantages of removal without damage were recognized, and little pieces of folded stamp edging or similar gummed paper were used as 'hinges'. Stamp hinges or mounts when first invented were probably little better, leaving pieces behind on both the stamp and the album page when removed. The true peelable hinge (**a**) as known today comes away cleanly when properly used (moistened lightly and to a minimum extent), but still leaves a minute film of gum on both stamp and page. A fetish for 'unmounted mint' grew up on the Continent after World War II. This means that unused stamps are unacceptable to some collectors if they have the very least mark left by a hinge, or the least crease or disturbance of their gum – with unfortunately a severe effect on saleability and value. Transparent pockets of plastic (**b**) are made by several manufacturers, either ready cut or in long strips for trimming to size, in which stamps are held sufficiently firmly. The back part, which can be either clear or black, is gummed for sticking to the album page. Thus the stamps can remain in pristine condition.

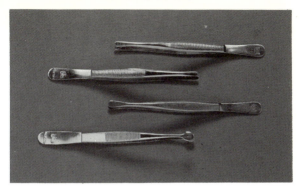

111 various styles of tweezers

There is less point in using these special mounts for used stamps, but many collectors do so in order to prevent stamp surfaces from rubbing on the opposite page, or because the black-margined kind shows up perforated edges to advantage.

All stamps, used or unused, should whenever possible be handled only with tweezers, of the special 'spade-ended' kind sold for the purpose.

For the mounting of whole envelopes or of 'cut-outs' bearing stamps and postmarks, ordinary photographic mounting corners are suitable. Transparent ones are preferable, and the old-fashioned gummed type will be found much more manageable than the self-adhesive variety. Sometimes it is desirable to display the back, which unless special 'cover' albums are used can be done by transparent 'pockets' bound in with ordinary leaves, by cutting holes in an ordinary page, by slitting the envelope on three sides and opening it out (not recommended for items of value) or (best of all) by making a photostat of the back and mounting it beneath.

STAMP COLLECTING

The removal of used stamps from paper is often a source of unnecessary worry. The great majority are perfectly safe to throw into a bowl of warm water to soak off. But the following should first be carefully set aside:

1. Any unused stamps accidentally included.
2. All paper bearing writing in ink; this should be cut off.
3. All stamps stuck on coloured paper. These need special treatment.
4. All coloured margins from air mail envelopes unless known to be 'fast'.
5. All stamps in fugitive inks. This particularly includes those British and colonial stamps of about 1880 to 1950 which contain purple printing.
6. All self-adhesive stamps. These cannot normally be removed at all but must be neatly cut out.
7. All stamps believed to have water-soluble print on or under the gum.
8. Finally, and very important, all stamps with interesting postmarks which it would be better to retain complete.

If stamps on paper in categories 2 to 5 are immersed they are likely not only to be spoilt themselves, but also to ruin others which they touch whilst wet.

After soaking for about five minutes the gum will in most cases be sufficiently dissolved. Some stamps and paper will by then have parted company in the water and should be picked out carefully with tweezers. The stamps should be laid face down on absorbent paper or cloth to dry. Any that have not parted should be carefully peeled apart, again using tweezers to handle the stamps. It is often important to preserve stamps in joined strips or blocks, which requires a very delicate touch when they are wet and consequently liable to fall apart at the perforations. The process of peeling them off can be done more safely if they are placed firmly face downwards, paper and all, on a flat absorbent surface whilst still wet and the backing then peeled away from the stamps, rather than vice versa.

Occasionally stamps will be found (usually Russian or Chinese) which remain stubbornly stuck. If the gum has not dissolved in water it can be assumed that nothing else is likely to loosen it without damaging the stamp, and the only course therefore is to abandon the attempt and to trim the paper neatly round the stamp and mount it like that. A 'thinned' stamp is practically valueless.

Stamps in classes 3 and 7 can be dealt with by the use of a **sweat box**. This is merely a small reasonably airtight container with a water-saturated pad of newspaper, blotting paper or similar substance in the base, and a 'platform' clear of it on which stamps can rest. The platform can be made from a small piece of perforated zinc, expanded aluminium grille or similar non-rusting 'open' material with the edges bent over to form 'legs'. The stamps, preferably one at a time, are shut in the box for a period ranging from ten minutes to as much as two days; their gum begins to dissolve in the moist atmosphere and they can then be peeled off as before. Only experiment and experience can dictate how long the process will take, but the main factor is the actual quantity of backing paper, for it is that which has to absorb the greatest amount of moisture before any loosening takes place. Occasional inspection is essential; premature attempts to peel off are bound to result in damage to the stamp, but if it is left too long any soluble ink will be affected, or even a mildew may be set up. A sweat box can also be used, but only with extreme care, for stamps with fugitive ink (class 5 above); as much as possible of the backing paper should be carefully removed first, so as to limit the exposure of the ink to moisture. It is very useful too for removing old mounts and other traces of paper from unused stamps; this can be quite quick, because the gum is largely exposed and liquefies surprisingly quickly. Very great care is then needed in handling to avoid further disturbance to the gum, and the tendency to curl up tightly when drying must be guarded against.

Used stamps with extraneous stains will often yield to boiling in water for a short period. Naturally this should not be inflicted on any with non-fast colours, but if the stamp is apparently rendered worthless by the stain, such drastic measures cannot make matters worse and may well restore it to perfect health!

STAMP COLLECTING

Writing up and arranging is much too big a subject to cover adequately here, but, in any case, whatever guide lines are set down there can be no compulsion to follow them. Both arranging and writing up are very individual aspects of collecting and can reflect the owner's personality and interests far more than his actual stamps. They are bound to develop as experience and skill grow, and they will probably be influenced by the opinions of friends and acquaintances.

The arranging of stamps depends on the story one wants to explore or tell. If the catalogue is followed exactly, it will be a matter of dividing the issues, as listed, into convenient groups to fit comfortably on to a page. For a straightforward 'country' collection many collectors find a strictly chronological sequence better because it avoids the need for re-mounting every time new denominations are added to a set and gives a clearer picture of postal rate and other changes. Some people collect only unused stamps, some only used ones, and some both. If both, they can be arranged as two distinct sets or with unused and used specimens side by side. 'Mixed' sets (**172**) are not regarded as very satisfactory but temporarily, at least, one may have to accept stamps in whatever form they come along, or according to the depth of one's purse.

A thematic collection offers much more freedom, as has been mentioned earlier in this chapter, and the number of stamps on a page is likely to be less, with more emphasis on the writing-up.

A page is likely to be neatest if it can be made symmetrical, though sometimes the sequence of shapes and sizes makes that impossible. As a rule, album pages are marked out with faint squares and the centre line is indicated. It should always be respected, and a standard spacing should be adopted and kept to: for example always one clear square between stamps in a row, always two clear squares between rows, and always five between one set and the next. Obviously that depends on the amount and size of writing up – but the writing ought if possible to be secondary to the stamps and not attempt to dominate them.

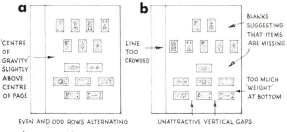

EVEN AND ODD ROWS ALTERNATING   UNATTRACTIVE VERTICAL GAPS

a) GOOD & b) BAD ARRANGEMENTS OF THE SAME STAMPS

A less regimented appearance is achieved if the number of stamps in a row alternates between odd and even. Blanks should of course be left for stamps yet to be acquired, but the arrangement should not give the impression of more blanks than there really are. For instance a set of seven stamps arranged as a row of five followed by a row of two may suggest that two are missing; it is far better to mount between four and three.

As with an ordinary printed page, it looks better if the 'weight' is nearer the top. The low 'centre of gravity' created when the number of stamps in each row increases towards the bottom is much less pleasant, though occasional lapses may be unavoidable and will provide variety. Some collectors like to experiment with 'fancy' arrangements – circles, crosses etc. – but this almost invariably detracts from the stamps themselves.

If a page is 'planned' at an early stage when only one or two stamps may be available for mounting, it is a good idea to jot down (either on the page itself or perhaps in a notebook kept for the purpose) what is intended for the remainder. It is only too easy to forget, to make a muddle, and to have to re-do the page.

116 a typical complete album page: the St Helena issue of 1961

WAYS TO COLLECT

a mapping pen produces thicker down- than up-strokes ∿

a 'stylograph' pen gives a uniform but less interesting thickness ∿

a ball-pointed pen can produce **variations** *in intensity* ⌇

so can a **pencil** *but it must be kept sharp and constantly turned*

examples of ~~joined~~ writing and <u>separated</u> letters

117 examples of writing-up

Writing up probably causes more worry than any other aspect of collecting – which partly explains the popularity of printed albums. Most people have a quite unnecessary feeling of inferiority about their handwriting and lettering, realizing that the kind of writing they would use for a letter is unsuited in size, style and colour for an album leaf. But this is more a question of method and materials, and anyone with a reasonably steady hand will find that with a fine pen (a mapping pen or possibly a modern draughtsman's 'stylograph' type of not more than 0.25 mm thickness) and black (**not** blue) drawing or fountain pen ink it is possible to produce a small neat version of ordinary handwriting which is perfectly acceptable. Even a black ball-point pen can produce a good result provided it is of 'fine' grade and has not become worn and blotchy. So will a very finely sharpened pencil, with the advantage that it can be rubbed out.

If joined-up writing looks untidy it is worth deliberately separating the letters and writing them one by one – but still in the forms one is accustomed to using, so that the result does not look unnatural and still 'flows' well.

When using a pen or pencil it is best to have the paper on a slightly resilient backing to make it easier to maintain a light even pressure. A page in an album, cushioned by other pages beneath, is better in that respect than one resting on a hard board; if in position in an ordinary spring-back album, however, it is unlikely to be flat enough for comfort or proper control.

HEADING DONE with BROAD NIB

THICKER 'Stylograph' PEN

DRY TRANSFER Letters

118 examples of album page headings

It is an advantage to 'rough out' the writing faintly in pencil before embarking on ink. Better still is to write in ink on a piece of loose paper so as to discover how much space will be occupied, and then to offer this against the space available. In this way the writing can be neatly centred on the stamps, and any danger of overrunning the space can be foreseen before it occurs and upsets the balance.

The temptation to use a wider pen should be resisted; except in very skilled hands the result will be much too black and overpowering. The only exception is for headings (such as the country name) where a bolder and perhaps slightly ornamental style may not be out of place. Alternatively stencil lettering may be tried, possibly of the dry-transfer kind.

A typewriter can be used, but great care is needed. To start with, direct typing on to a page has to be done before the stamps are finally mounted, and must therefore be extremely carefully planned. Separately typed 'labels' stuck on are liable to be messy. The amount of space occupied by typing is greater than one might expect, and the danger of the stamps being overwhelmed is even more than with manuscript lettering.

Whatever method of writing up is adopted, it is important to be consistent; so if first attempts are condemned after a period of experiment they should in due course be re-done, even if it means wasting some pages and re-mounting the stamps. After that (unless perhaps some pages are to be prepared for a special purpose) it is best to stick closely to one size, style, spacing and type of pen.

Some other **accessories** to collecting have already been mentioned above. **Tweezers** are essential for cutting down the handling that stamps receive, and once the facility for using them has been gained they will be found invaluable for sorting loose stamps, quickly and without danger of damage. **Perforation gauges** are described in Chapter 3. To some collectors they are indispensable; to others they are of little interest. The same applies to **colour guides**; to many people the design is what matters and the exact colour is of no consequence. Colour is a subject as fraught with difficulties in stamps as it is in textiles, paints or artists' colours. No two systems of names or numbering agree, and no scientific basis of description could ever be practicable or even desirable for stamps. Sometimes an almost imperceptibly subtle change, not recordable on a colour guide, is an important differentiation between printings; more often simple 'red', 'blue' or 'green' are adequate. Published colour guides are helpful to those unsure of the differences between carmine and scarlet, or greenish blue and ultramarine, but they cannot possibly cover every stamp in the catalogue nor, conversely, can a catalogue publisher expect every new stamp to match one of a set of standard tints, however many there are.

A **magnifying glass** is one of the first accessories a collector will like to have, even if his eyesight is excellent. Many kinds are on the market, the most useful being the small folding type which can be constantly carried in the pocket and is occasionally handy for other purposes. The big reading-glass kind does not usually give sufficient magnification for stamps; better for home or desk use are the tripod kind or, if it can be afforded, the illuminated type incorporating a battery in the handle.

Watermark detectors have also been mentioned in Chapter 3. It is doubtful whether expenditure on them is justified – nor on the chalky paper detector which is only a piece of silver in the form of a 'pencil' tip and for which a real silver coin is an effective substitute.

7. VALUES AND PRICES

As with any commodity, the value of stamps depends on supply and demand. **Supply** usually means the quantity printed and available for sale and may, in the case of a stamp in current use, be increasing all the time. In the case of an obsolete stamp the quantity printed may be exactly known but, if not, it is still a factor which will not change. On the other hand the **demand** may change for any one of a number of reasons, principally concerned with popularity. Countries and groups and themes drift into and out of favour. Andorra (**a**) and Liechtenstein (**b**) were once unpopular. Now their older stamps are so much sought that their value has risen at a far greater rate than the average for Europe as a whole. The Saar (**c**) and Dominica (**d**) were, within the writer's recollection, popular. The former is a 'dead' country owing to political changes, and the latter has lost its following as a result of a postal régime which produces an excess of new issues. In both cases the effect on values is marked.

Supply and demand can both be 'manipulated'. It is not unknown for a speculator to purchase almost the entire printing of one value of a new series and then to sell them at a profit to those otherwise unable to complete their sets. Attempts are even made to monopolize the supply and force up the price of older issues by continually repeated offers to buy. Rarities and errors can be reprinted at will by unscrupulous printers or by the postal authorities themselves (an example of the latter is the USA 'Hammarskjöld' commemorative of 1962, of which a sheet with inverted centres was inadvertently sold (**a**)).

Artificial attempts to influence demand are made by agencies controlling new issues, and by advertiser-dealers in their wake. The commercial world of stamps, like those of toys, films and clothes, can only keep up its momentum and its earning capacity by constantly manufacturing a demand for something new; it would hardly occur to anyone to collect commemoratives of this satellite or that royal baby if advertisements did not stimulate a demand. Unfortunately it also may not always occur to buyers that stamps of these kinds (**b**) may quickly become about as much in demand as yesterday's newspaper or last season's women's fashions.

a   b

c   d

External influences on demand include politics and news; for example many more people became interested in the stamps of Rhodesia (**a**) and the Falklands (**b**) when they were in the headlines. Another factor is 'money supply'. When a national currency is weak the demand for negotiable goods like gold and paintings is high, and stamps follow suit; but, conversely, in conditions of prosperity there may still be increased demand from those with money to invest locally, as has been seen to occur in places like Japan (**c**) and Singapore (**d**).

Investment in stamps is certainly no safer than most other forms, and it is not to be recommended for the inexperienced. It is not one of the primary reasons for collecting, though it is true to say that one of the advantages of stamps over many other hobbies is that purchases do, on the average, tend to increase in value. The rates of increase, however, fluctuate enormously. As an example a stamp can be taken which has been much used by

investors and speculators, the British £1 of 1913 (**a**). This went off sale after only a few years, so 1913 can be regarded as a starting date. By 1967 it was fetching £90 at auction, which represents an average increase of $8\frac{1}{2}$% per annum. In 1980 the value (in unused, unmounted condition) had risen to around £4,000, a further gain of 34% per annum for 13 years. But the early 1984 value was only £1,500. That still represents 18% since 1967 (or nearly 11% over its whole life) but clearly anyone who bought at the 1980 figure had a bitter experience.

An unused Penny Black is worth about £2,000, an average gain by compound interest of – surprisingly – only $9\frac{1}{2}$% per annum since 1840.

It is always considered that the 'classic' stamps, i.e. those issued before about 1860 (**b, c**), are the safest investment of all. But as in the stock market there will always be those who aim higher and are prepared to take risks. One half of their flair is the ability to foresee increased demands and short supplies, while the equally important other half is the successful judgment of the right time to sell. Collectors play little direct part in this kind of thing but are, rightly or wrongly, caught up in its repercussions. To them the exact current market value of any one series is of little consequence, whereas to dealers it may be vital in determining their margin of profit, and they will use their specialist knowledge of a group to further their efforts to buy as cheaply as possible.

STAMP COLLECTING

The collector's specialist knowledge, or even his overall knowledge of stamps, may go much deeper than a dealer's. A dealer's position is different. His time is money, and he cannot afford to examine every stamp passing through his hands in the same detail as a collector can. So collectors, once they have got to know a particular field, always find it worth while to be on the look-out for the unusual which others may not have noticed. 'Bargain-hunting' in stamps has been decried, not because any degree of dishonesty is involved, but because there is the ever-present danger that what looks at first sight like a bargain is for some reason not what it appears. It is only too easy to mis-identify a watermark or to overlook a blemish. Nevertheless, even amongst stamps already searched through by dealers or other collectors, it is often possible to find varieties of watermark or perforation or design or such things as inverted or double surcharges, lurking unnoticed – not rarities perhaps, but valued, if one is reasonably fortunate, in pounds rather than pence. Occasionally a bit of a gamble is necessary. The writer recalls a 'schoolboy' album bought for very little which contained a used Trinidad & Tobago 5 shillings of George V, firmly stuck down; it might well have been defective, but the delicate operation of removing it after purchase was successful. Another find was a high-value Netherlands stamp sold by a dealer for next to nothing because it was very badly stained; when subjected to the boiling treatment described in Chapter 6 it emerged as a first-rate specimen. Time is money, and in either of those cases the rescue operation (whether successful or not) would have had to be measured against his own hours by a dealer, had he been the purchaser.

Selling, as everyone knows, is a different matter from buying. Stamps are the kind of commodity which can lie idle in a dealer's stock for a long while, and unless a particular section of the market is especially active, or he happens to know an immediate buyer, he will have to allow in his buying offers for the amount of time his capital may be tied up. In boom periods dealers may be noticed announcing that they are prepared to buy back what they are selling, at any future time. Such inducements to 'invest' should be treated with great caution; moreover the more sensational the offer to sell, the less likely it is that *any* dealer will buy back at *any* time at *any* price. Inevitably one must return to the fact that the 'classics' are the safest for those who are more interested in investment than in stamps *as* stamps. Nevertheless there is plenty of security too in the more easily acquired issues of the later 19th and early 20th century.

Catalogue values are dealers' selling prices and have to include all their overheads and 'handling charges'. Stamps are frequently offered at a fraction of catalogue price ('half cat.' is common). This does not imply profiteering by the catalogue publishers, who have to include all the overheads involved in maintaining a large and accessible stock. In the case of higher priced stamps and those in most demand the catalogue prices may be nearer the true value (and may even be below it), but they will still only be selling, not buying prices. So the catalogue value attached to a collection, accurate though it may be arithmetically, can be very misleading in being considerably above the total of current selling prices, which are themselves many times what might be offered by a dealer in the event of a quick sale being needed. Yet it is a reliable guide, provided also that careful attention is paid to **condition**.

To be worth full price a stamp must be in perfect condition, and there are numerous kinds of defect which may make it fall short – sometimes to the point of being uncollectable. A few very old and very rare stamps, however, hardly exist at all without some defects, and have to be accepted as they are. Conversely, a very old stamp in exceptional condition may be worth much more than catalogue value; the same applies to older stamps on their original envelopes.

Major defects include any kind of stain, tear, crease or fold or, worse, a piece missing altogether. The surface should not have been 'rubbed' to cause visible damage to the design, nor should the colour be faded or the back thinned. An unused stamp should not have lost its gum, and a used one should not have a very heavy or a non-postal cancellation. Most collectors would refuse to buy any stamp with one or more such defects.

What some would call minor defects experienced collectors might regard as far worse – particularly when applied to modern stamps. These include inaccurate centring (of the design in relation to the perforations (**a**)), one or more blunt perforation teeth (**b**), blemishes in the gum, or even a slogan cancellation (**c**) instead of a neat circular one. Slight imperfections of these kinds will affect the value, and anyone who does not mind them may well be happy to pay a lower price to fill a space on the album page.

Some of the descriptions of condition used for stamps may be a little puzzling. 'Un' and 'us' merely mean unused and used, and are the normal headings of price columns in a catalogue. 'Mint' means unused, in the condition originally bought at a post office, though probably showing signs of having been mounted; 'Unmounted mint' ('un m') does not mean 'not mounted now', but *'never* mounted'; the demand for stamps in this condition (what the Germans graphically call *'postfrisch'*) has been mentioned in the last chapter. 'OG' means 'original gum', implying that it is present but incomplete; applied to an older stamp it indicates that it has not been doctored by re-gumming. 'GD' means 'gum disturbed' or could be interpreted as 'gum defective'. 'CTO' means 'cancelled to order' (**25**) (see Chapter

2). 'Used' (**a**), 'fine used' (**b**) ('fu') and 'superb used' (**c**) can be interpreted how one wishes; beauty is in the eye of the beholder or, in the case of stamps that of the vendor, who may be over-enthusiastic in his claims! 'On cover' or 'on entire' are generally accepted as meaning used on any kind of original envelope, wrapper or folded letter, whereas 'on piece' implies a piece neatly cut from such an envelope. 'FDC' is short for 'first day cover'.

Auction catalogues and dealers' lists contain numerous abbreviations like the above, often with a series of symbols for 'mint', 'used' etc. which are explained in a key. They also normally carry references to 'cat. nos' (catalogue numbers) which in Britain usually means Stanley Gibbons' catalogue. Often such a reference merely reads, for example, 'SG20', which means no. 20 in Gibbons' list. 'High cat.' is jargon for 'high catalogue value' and carries slight undertones of wishful thinking. 'Perf' (sometimes just 'P') means 'perforated', usually followed by the gauge number, and 'Wmk' means 'watermark'. 'MS' means 'miniature sheet' (**26**, **29**), as opposed to 'm/s' which might be applied to a 'manuscript' postal marking.

8. AIDS TO IDENTIFICATION

The identification of stamps becomes progressively more difficult as the years go on, and even the most experienced collector sometimes finds it extremely hard to locate a strange stamp in the catalogue. He is unlikely to stumble very often over the country of origin; the biggest problems arise with countries like France, Spain, Italy and most of the 'Iron Curtain' countries, which in the past 40 years or so have issued vast numbers of stamps of fairly consistent character. However, some guide lines will be suggested later in this chapter.

Confronted with a mixed lot, the beginner will do best to start by setting aside in separate piles the countries which he can identify readily, leaving for the present any inscribed with characters or alphabets he does not understand. Many, like Canada, France and Portugal, are self-explanatory.

British stamps, by world-wide consent, are permitted to omit the country-name and to rely for identification on the sovereign's head. The so-called 'country' stamps show the lion, dragon, and shield with hand emblems of Scotland (**a**), Wales (**b**) and Northern Ireland (**c**) respectively (for reasons best understood by the Post Office, England is not permitted her own distinctive stamps).

AIDS TO IDENTIFICATION

The following table, which runs geographically round each continent in turn, will help towards identifying the principal territory names in their own languages on stamps, as well as those which have changed their names. Those in the Greek or Cyrillic alphabets are given in capitals (as is usual on stamps). Some names differing only by one or two letters are ignored; so are rarities and very minor stamp-issuing states.

Europe

Éire	Ireland (**42e**)
Island	Iceland (**145a**)
Suomi	Finland (**32d**)
Itä Karjala	Eastern Karelia (**a**)
Norge, Noreg	Norway (**37b, 80, 81, 89**)
Sverige	Sweden (**42a, 62c, 85b**)
Danmark	Denmark (**73a–c, 97e**)
Føroyar	Faroe Islands (**b**)
Deutschland, Deutsche Post etc.	Germany (**63c, 68f, 85c, 145d–f**)
Deutsche Bundespost	West Germany (**c, 35a**)
DDR, Deutsche Demokratische Republik	East Germany (**d, 23a**)
Bayern	Bavaria (**e**)
Preussen	Prussia (**f**)

STAMP COLLECTING

Braunschweig	Brunswick (**a**)
Sachsen	Saxony (**b**)
Norddeutscher Postbezirk	North German Postal Confederation (**c**)
S.O. (Silésie Orientale)	Eastern Silesia (**d**)
C.G.H.S., Haute Silésie	Upper Silesia (**60d**)
Nederland	Holland (**42d, 62d, 146d–e**)
R.F., République Française	France (**2a, 19, 66d, 79d–e**)
España, Republica Española	Spain (**2e, 6f, 101d–e**)
A.M.G.V.G. or A.M.G.F.T.T.	Allied Military Government of Venezia Giulia or Free Territory of Trieste (**127b**)
S.T.T., Trst	Trieste (**e**)
Venezia Tridentina	Trentino
Franco Bollo	'Postage Stamp' – used in several Italian states (**24d**)
Helvetia, Confoederatio Helvetica	Switzerland (**26, 72b–d, 150a–b**)
Österreich, K.K. Post	Austria (**79a, 100c, 150c–f, 152c**)
Kärnten, G.K.C.	Carinthia (**f**)
Ceskoslovensko	Czechoslovakia (**5e, 36d**)
Böhmen und Mähren	Bohemia and Moravia
Slovensko	Slovakia
Magyar Posta etc.	Hungary (**29, 36e, 54a–b**)
S.H.S., Kraljevstvo Srba Hrvata i Slovenaca	Yugoslavia (**g**)
Hrvatska	Croatia (**g, 152b**)

Drzava, Co.Ci. (Commissariato Civile)	Slovenia (**a**)
ЦРНА ГОРА (Crna Gora)	Montenegro (**b**)
СРБИЈА	Serbia (**152a**)
Shqiperia etc.	Albania (**97l, 127a, 152e–f**)
Hellas, ΕΛΛΑΣ	Greece (**3d, 40a, 61a, 153a**)
ΗΠΕΙΡΟΣ	Epirus
ΙΟΝΙΚΟΝ ΚΡΑΤΟΣ	Ionian Islands (**c**)
ΘΡΑΚΗΣ	Thrace
Σ.Δ.Δ.	Dodecanese Islands
ΣΑΜΟΥ	Samos
ΛΗΜΝΟΣ	Lemnos
ΚΡΗΤΗ	Crete (**88**)
БЪЛГАРИЯ	Bulgaria (**6e, 25b, 153b**)
Polska	Poland
Generalgouvernement	Poland (**d**)
Srodkowa Litwa	Central Lithuania
РОССІЯ, Р.С.Ф.С.Р., С.С.С.Р.	Russia (**2b, 49f, 101c, 153c**)
ПОЧТА, ПОЧТОВАЯ МАРКА	'Postage', 'Postage Stamp' (Russia) (**79b**)
Lietuva	Lithuania (**f**)
Klaipėda	Memel
Latvija	Latvia (**e**)
Eesti	Estonia (**g**)
Inkeri	Ingermanland (**h**)
УКРАÏНСКА …	Ukraine (**58a**)
ДАЛЬНЕ-ВОСТОЧНАЯ	Far Eastern Republic
Emp. Ottoman	Turkey

131

STAMP COLLECTING

ASIA

Liban	Lebanon (**126a**)
Arabie Saoudite, S.A.K.	Saudi Arabia (**a**)
Y.A.R.	Yemen Arab Republic (**b**)
Poste Persane	Iran (**24b**)
Établissements Français dans l'Inde	French India (**156e**)
Ceylon	Sri Lanka (**21e**, **79c**, **156a**)
КИТАЙ (Cathay)	China (Russian P.Os) (**c**)
Nippon	Japan
Filipinas, Pilipinas	Philippines (**157c–e**)
Cambodge, République Khmere	Kampuchea
Siam	Thailand
North Borneo	Sabah (**25a**)
Nederlandsch Indië	Indonesia (**141c**)

AUSTRALASIA

Deutsch-Neu-Guinea, N.W. Pacific Islands	New Guinea (**d**)
New Hebrides, Nouvelles Hebrides	Vanuatu
Nouvelle Calédonie	New Caledonia (**161a**)
Toga	Tonga (**e**)
Établissements Français de l'Océanie	French Polynesia (**161b**)
Gilbert & Ellice Islands	Kiribati and Tuvalu

AMERICA

Grønland	Greenland (**145b**)
Mejico	Mexico (**24e**)
British Honduras	Belize (**7d**)
Curaçao	Netherlands Antilles
British Guiana	Guyana
Guyane Française	French Guiana
Montevideo	Uruguay (**a**)

ANTARCTICA

Terres Australes et Antarctiques Françaises	French Antarctic Territory (**165b**)

AFRICA

Açores	Azores (**165e**)
Maroc, Marruecos, Marokko	Morocco (**170d–e**)
L.A.R.	Libya (**b**)
Territoire Française des Afars et des Issas, Côte Française des Somalis	Djibouti (**59c**)
E.A.F.	East African Forces (**c**)
M.E.F.	Middle East Forces (**d**)
A.O.I., Africa Orientale Italiana	Italian East Africa (**e**)
Benadir	Somalia (**f**)
Oltre Giuba	Jubaland (**g**)

STAMP COLLECTING

British East Africa	Kenya (**53d**)
Deutsch-Ostafrika, N.F., G.E.A.	German East Africa, Tanganyika (**a, b**)
Companhia do Nyassa	Nyassa Company (**c**)
Madagascar, République Malgache	Malagasy Republic
Archipel des Comores	Comoro Islands
C.F.A. (Colonie Française Africaine)	Réunion (**d**)
British Central Africa, B.C.A., Nyasaland	Malaŵi (**e**)
British South Africa Company	Rhodesia (N. and S.) (**f, 122a**)
Northern Rhodesia	Zambia
Southern Rhodesia	Zimbabwe (**167b**)
Zuid Afrika, Suid-Afrika, R.S.A.	South Africa (**2d, 92a, 97c**)
Zuid Afrikaansche Republiek	Transvaal (**60c, 75d**)
Oranje Vrij Staat	Orange River Colony
G (on Cape of Good Hope)	Griqualand West
Basutoland	Lesotho
Bechuanaland	Botswana (**20b**)
Deutsch-Südwestafrika, Zuid-West Afrika, Suidwes-Afrika, S.W.A.	South-West Africa (**33a**)

AIDS TO IDENTIFICATION

État Independant du Congo, Congo Belge, Belgisch Congo, République Democratique du Congo	Zaïre (**67d**)
Est Africain Allemand Occupation Belge, A.O.	Ruanda-Urundi (**a**)
Congo Français, Afrique Équatoriale Française	French Equatorial Africa
Moyen Congo, République du Congo	Congo
Oubangui-Chari, République Centrafricaine	Central African Republic
Rio Muni, Guinea Española	Equatorial Guinea (**b**)
S.T(h)omé (e Principe)	St Thomas and Prince (**c**)
Kamerun	Cameroun (**d**)
Dahomey	Bénin
Haute Volta	Burkina Faso
Gold Coast	Ghana (**166a**)
Côte d'Ivoire	Ivory Coast (**170f**)
Guinée (Française)	Guinea (**5c**)
Guiné (Portugueza)	Guinea-Bissau (**e**)
Sénégambie et Niger, Haut-Sénégal et Niger, Soudan Français	Mali
Cabo Verde	Cape Verde Islands
Afrique Occidentale Française	French West Africa
Sahara Español	Spanish Sahara
Cabo Juby	Cape Juby

The residue, with country name in other alphabets or none at all, is likely to include some of the following, which are taken in a similar order:

Postage due stamps of the Netherlands or one of her colonies, inscribed 'Te Betalen' (**a**).

Pre-World War I stamps of Turkey, identifiable by the 'toughra' or Sultan's formal signature (**67b**).

Stamps of the Arab Kingdom of Syria (1920) (**b**).

Stamps of Hejaz (**c**) and Nejd, combined in 1926 to become Saudi Arabia; some of these also bear a 'toughra'.

Earlier and a few later stamps of Iran (**d**), bearing a lion with scimitar and rising sun.

Issues of some of the Indian Native States, many of them very primitive in character and inscribed only in local scripts (**e**).

Earlier stamps of Nepal (**f**).

Issues of China and of her many provinces. Ordinary Chinese stamps are distinguishable by the character 中 in a main inscription of (usually) six characters (**g**, **24f**, **51b**). This equally applies to stamps of Taiwan; both those and stamps of mainland China may be inscribed 'Republic of China'.

Stamps of Manchuria under Japanese rule, with the five-pointed propeller-like 'Kaoliang' emblem (**a**).

Stamps of Mongolia, with the symbol like four crowns around a circle (**b**).

Stamps of Korea, those of the South (**d**) (and of the former Empire) usually bearing the 'Yin-yang' symbol ⊘ and those of the North (**c**) by the last but one character ♀ of the inscription.

Issues of Japan, the earlier ones with the Imperial sixteen-petalled chrysanthemum and the later with the character ⊟ in the inscription (**21a**, **93b**, **122c**, **157b**).

Issues of Ryukyu Islands like those of Japan in appearance but with the character 王内 (**e**).

Early issues of Thailand, finely engraved stamps with the King's head facing left (**f**).

Early issues of Brazil, merely numerals on a patterned background (**h**).

Modern issues of Libya with all inscriptions except the denomination in Arabic characters, bearing a striped shield and an eagle (**g**).

A knowledge of the Greek and Cyrillic alphabets as used in Eastern Europe is helpful, as well as the numerals associated with the Arabic. However this is only a very preliminary step towards understanding the languages, and the tables that follow can be no more than a guide towards deciphering postmarks and simple inscriptions. The Arabic alphabet, with its many forms of each letter according to their position in the word, is beyond the scope of this book; few collectors really need to learn it or any of the innumerable other Eastern scripts.

GREEK		CYRILLIC	GREEK		CYRILLIC
A	A	А	P	R	Р
B	B	Б	Σ	S	С
		В	T	T	Т
Γ	G	Г	Υ	U	У
Δ	D	Д	Φ	F	Ф
E	Ĕ	Е	X	KH	Х
	ZH	Ж		TS	Ц
Z	Z	З		CH	Ч
H	Ē			SH	Ш
Θ	TH			SHCH	Щ
I	I	И		HARDENING	Ъ
K	K	К		Υ	Ы
Λ	L	Л		SOFTENING	Ь
M	M	М	E		Э
N	N	Н		YU	Ю
Ξ	X			YA	Я
O	Ŏ	О	Ψ	PS	
Π	P	П	Ω	Ō	

138 Greek and Cyrillic alphabets

The problems of actual identification of stamps in the catalogue when their country is known have already been touched upon. Experience is the long-term solution but it is surprising how quickly anyone reasonably well acquainted with the subject can 'date' a stamp and find it in the catalogue list. The following methods are useful to the less knowledgeable:

1. Some catalogue lists have a 'design key'. If the subject can be identified – or the reason for the stamp's issue – the key will give the catalogue number or at any rate a list of possibilities.

2. The currency of a country may have changed at some time (like British old pence ('d.') to new pence ('p') That may help to narrow the field (**a, b**).

3. Denominations of stamps constantly change as postal rates change, especially when inflation is high. It is therefore often helpful to search amongst listings where the particular denomination frequently occurs. For example Britain used $8\frac{1}{2}$p. stamps for first-class letters only in 1975–77.

4. The styles of country names occasionally change. For example 'R.S.A.' as an abbreviation for 'Republic of South Africa' or of its equivalent in Afrikaans only occurs from 1967 onwards (**2d**).

5. The artistic appearance of stamps changes with current fashions and the subject matter with social and political and other influences. These, often the best guides to the expert, are nevertheless the most intangible to explain. Under this heading would also come changes in monarchs' portraits, which make the dating of British Commonwealth stamps moderately easy (**a**).

6. Linked with the last, the work of various printers is often readily distinguishable and limited to certain periods. Stamps printed in photogravure are unlikely to be earlier than the 1920s (**b**), while multi-coloured stamps printed by any of the processes will almost certainly date from the 1950s or later.

7. Quite often a commemorative stamp actually bears the date of the anniversary or event it marks (**c**). Sometimes this may have to be deduced; for example a man's birth and death dates may be given as 1615–1680, from which one may assume that the stamp may have commemorated the third centenary (in 1980) of his death or the 350th anniversary (in 1965) of his birth. If both fail, there is no harm in continuing the catalogue search for the subsequent year or two, for belated commemorations are by no means unknown. But the dates may not actually mark an anniversary at all, in which case one must look further afield.

8. To an increasing extent, postal authorities recognize the

a

b

c

problem (after all, it is largely of their own making) and incorporate the year figures into each design. Canada began the practice (perhaps not solely with collectors in mind) in 1935 with 'secret' dates hidden in the designs and detectable only with a magnifier (**a**). At the other extreme, Brazil and Ecuador have in recent years printed the last two numerals of the year as large as their own country names (**b**).

9. If the stamp has been used, the date may be visible in the postmark (**c**). Then the search should start in the lists at that date and work backwards.

10. If the catalogue search is done by means of the illustrations it should be remembered that all the designs in one series are unlikely to be shown and that they may vary considerably, even in shape and size. Also it is easy to be misled by reproductions of multi-coloured stamps; a red and green flag on a grey background, for example may look totally different in a monochrome reproduction, and it may be better to look for a smaller but clearer feature as the 'key' for a search.

11. Often there are several series in a single or similar designs, sometimes scattered through several pages of listings covering a number of years. Usually cross-references are provided in such cases and they should be checked, particularly if the first attempt at identification seems to lead to a stamp of unexpectedly high price!

9. SUGGESTED SUBJECTS AND MISCELLANEOUS TOPICS

The preceding chapters contain plenty of suggestions as to the lines that a collection may take. This final one consists mostly of a roam round the world of stamps with some pointers to the pitfalls and pleasures.

British stamps alone are a wide enough field for many people. To acquire a Penny Black (**53b**) and its companion the Two Pence Blue (**a**) of 1840 is a natural ambition, but even the former will now cost £30 or more for a reasonably nice specimen. Subsequent issues of Queen Victoria are bedevilled by the great proportion of bad postmarks – the 'killer' cancellations that were employed almost throughout the reign to prevent the re-use of used stamps (**b**). So the assembly of a good-looking collection, even in used condition, is a long and expensive task, and completion is impossible because of the number of rarities

and high values (**142c**). Nevertheless the line-engraved penny stamps (and to a less extent the halfpenny (**142e**), three-halfpence and twopence) are a popular and inexhaustible field for specialists, who identify the flaws and markings on individual stamps and allocate them to their numbered plates. This task is aided by the corner letters on every stamp which indicate its position on the original sheet, and in the later issues by the plate number itself printed on the stamps (**142d**, **143a**). The unlikelihood of finding two stamps exactly alike is as much a challenge to some as it is daunting to others. The more heavily cancelled specimens can be turned to good use as a fruitful source for 'numeral' postmarks, which can be collected in three series: English and Welsh (**142b**), Scottish (**143b**), and Irish (**143c**) ('Ireland' at that time comprised the whole country). Then, for those with a deeper purse, there are the 'used abroads', collectable as single loose stamps (**73f**) but very much preferable on piece or on cover.

Edward VII 'GB' are few in basic numbers but numerous and complex to those who enjoy separating the many different printings and shades (**d**). To a lesser degree the same applies to the next reign, that of George V, which saw the famous 'Sea Horses' high values (**123a**) as well as the Postal Union Congress issue of 1929 with its beautiful £1 value (**e**).

Some collectors like the 'control numbers' on many of these issues – marginal markings indicating the year of printing (**92b**). 1934 saw the introduction of photogravure, which thereafter was used for most stamps with the exception of the higher denominations; a GB collection starting at that point would stand a good chance of completion, particularly if, initially, varieties of watermark and phosphor lines are ignored. It would include almost all the commemoratives as well as the 'Machin' series still current at the time of writing, which has expanded into the longest ever known (**1a**, **b**). It would also include the separate 'country' issues for Northern Ireland, Scotland and Wales (**128**).

The comparatively modern separate stamps of Jersey (**a**), Guernsey (**b**), Alderney and the Isle of Man (**c**) are an attractive group commencing only in 1969 and later. Such a collection can be supplemented, if one feels inclined, by finding older ordinary British issues with the appropriate postmarks. Similar remarks apply to the stamps of Ireland; these contain few rarities apart from the high values, and the first issues were British stamps with overprints (**63a**).

The **Scandinavian** group, comprising Iceland (**a**), Norway (**37b**), Sweden (**85b**), Denmark (**97e**), Finland (**40d**), Greenland (**b**), and latterly the Faroe (**129b**) and Åland Islands, is one of the most attractive groups. A large proportion of all their issues is recess-printed, almost a guarantee of popularity. The very early issues are now beyond most people's pockets, and so are unused specimens of many of the 'middle' ones, but used collections of all except the island groups and Greenland can readily be got together.

German issues are likely to be found in great numbers by the beginner, to whom the very profusion of cheap stamps is an obvious incentive. They need to be divided into quite a number of groups, beginning at the present day with West and East German (see Chapter 8) and the separate West German issues for West Berlin (**3e**). Immediately after World War II there were numerous issues for the various occupied zones (**c**). Prior to that were the stamps of Hitler's Germany (**d**), preceded by those of the Weimar republic (**e**) and those of the Kaisers (**f**) back to 1871, when the country was united from numerous small states. Most of these had issued stamps (some of them in various confederations), and those of Bavaria (**129e**) and Württemberg continued till the 1920s. Some are thus comparatively cheap, but the majority – from places like Hannover (**g**), Saxony and Schleswig-Holstein – are scarce and expensive.

The **Benelux** countries can be considered together. Of the three, perhaps Luxembourg is the most collectable by virtue of having issued fewer stamps (**a**), and Belgium the least for the opposite reason (**b**). Belgium has long tended to have too many charity stamps with too high premiums (**c**), as well as large numbers of railway parcels (**65d**) and similar issues which, though mostly inexpensive, are dull and unpopular. The aesthetic quality of Netherlands stamps is much higher and they enjoy great popularity (**d, e**).

France, as might be expected, is an enormous country in the philatelic sense, and to commence a would-be complete collection from scratch would be to undertake the impossible. Nevertheless much interest and enjoyment can still be obtained even from the classic (pre-1876) issues if one is prepared to disregard the rarer items and to concentrate on shades, postmarks and minor varieties of the commoner ones (**f**). The 'modern' issues (i.e. from about 1930 onwards) include hundreds of different line-engraved designs, most of them priced in pence rather than pounds – particularly in used condition, for they are, for the most part, stamps for real use and not produced only for the pleasure of collectors. It is an attractive idea to collect them in some way other than chronologically – perhaps grouping the

landscapes of different departments (**173**), inventors and inventions, cathedrals (**b**), and so on. In between the classic and the modern is a less spectacular group of, mostly, small-sized definitives (**66d**), which continue as a sort of secondary streak through the catalogue lists right up to the present day and occasionally produce real masterpieces of design (**a**, **2a**).

Monaco's stamps are mostly produced for collectors and have many of the characteristics of French. The quantity of low denominations (**c**) enables a flying start to be made at minimal cost but there is little of philatelic 'depth' (**d**). **Andorra** is somewhat different, with concurrent issues under the post offices of France (**97f**) and Spain (**e**), and only a moderate output of commemoratives; their great popularity has however forced prices out of the range of collectors of modest means.

Spain is less popular than France. The 19th century issues have much less appeal, and contain too many expensive items to be recommended as a collecting field. Those of 1900 to 1950 are mostly humdrum too, but do include the complex Civil War issues, which contain much for the postal historian. From 1950 onwards a very limited variety of definitives has been accompanied by great numbers of special issues, some of them in long-drawn-out series and mostly of low face value; they are a source of much interest to thematic collectors (**2e**).

Portugal too has a great deal to offer (**82d**), though proliferations of special issues in the 1920s and in the last decade or so have not endeared her to collectors. The earliest issues are very expensive and hard to find in reasonable condition.

Gibraltar's stamps follow the usual kind of British colonial pattern (**a**). Her great popularity stems from being not only British but also part of Europe, and is reflected in rising prices. Her modern issues, though colourful, unfortunately rate low in standard of design. **Malta** has been more fortunate in that respect (**b**), and has always maintained a staunch independence of standard kinds of design from colonial times onwards. Those of **Cyprus** have become more and more Greek in character (**92f**) with, more recently, separate issues for the Turkish parts (**c**).

Most stamps are popular in their own country, and none more so than in **Italy**. Her population and commerce are great enough to make the ordinary stamps quite plentiful (**a**). Historically they closely parallel German, commencing with many separate states, continuing with usually well-designed unified issues, blossoming out in the 1920s and 1930s with pictorials which culminated in the rather excessive productions of the Fascist era, undergoing the austere end-of-war period of 1943–45 (**36f**) when various fragmented areas again had their own stamps, and finally providing a veritable flood of special issues – usually as single stamps but at the most in sets of three or four. Add to these a considerable variety of ancillary series – postage dues parcel post stamps (**65e**), special delivery stamps (**64c**) etc. – as well as plenty of potential philatelic study in many of the definitives, a leavening of higher-priced stamps, and the fascinations of the 'used abroad' and military campaigns, and it will be seen that there is enough for a lifetime's interest. Many of the early (pre-1862) stamps of the states are costly (**5a**, **123b**) and abound in reprints and forgeries, but they can be ignored. Two independent states, **San Marino** (**b**) and the **Vatican City** (**c**), still exist and are popular with collectors – the latter particularly with those with an interest in stamps with a religious theme. However neither can any longer be wholeheartedly recommended because the earlier issues are so expensive.

Switzerland is one of the favourite countries of all – largely because of her moderate new issue policy and because of her first-rate designs (**a**, **b**). Swiss stamp design is an art in its own right, not merely a reduced version of the art of printing or of posters. True, many older issues are out of the reach of the ordinary collector, but anyone of modest means can not only get together an attractive showing but will also find much of deeper interest. **Liechtenstein** (**120b, 171**) aims to obtain part of her national revenue from collectors, but the price increases amongst her older issues, like those of the other small states of Europe, are a deterrent to beginners.

Austria has a very large number of cheap stamps (**c**) – encouraging to those who want to swell their albums quickly – but also a dauntingly big proportion of expensive ones, particularly from the years before and after World War II. Some modern issues are masterpieces of engraving (**e**), and well worth collecting and studying for that reason alone, but the styles of design have become too diverse to appeal as much as they once did. The rather dull 19th century stamps (**d**) and the numerous issues for Bosnia (**39c**), the Field Post (**f**) and the various military occupations also offer much scope.

Czechoslovakia is the first East European country in this review and it shares with all the others an enormous output of commemorative and thematic issues of all kinds (**a**, **100b**), many of them available in cheap, cancelled-to-order form. However her stamp designers and engravers possess by far the greatest artistic flair, and for that reason her stamps can be highly recommended to anyone whose interests lean in that direction, while those who prefer deeper philatelic study can collect the pre-1919 Austrian and Hungarian 'forerunners' (**b**) and the inter-war issues (**36d**).

Hungary also used Austrian, or rather Austro-Hungarian, stamps for many years. Her own up to the 1930s are numerous, cheap and not specially attractive (**c**); neither they nor the subsequent mass of pictorial issues (**e**) can really be recommended, though there are small pockets of interest like the strange inflation issues of 1945–46 with their astronomical denominations up to 500,000,000,000,000,000 pengös (**d**).

Yugoslavia ought to be collected as a whole – i.e. together with the formerly separate states of Montenegro (**131b**) and Serbia (**a**), the Austrian issues for Bosnia (**39c**), and the various other interesting issues for territories like Slovenia (**131a**) and German-occupied Croatia (**b**). The disputed areas of Trieste (**130e**), Lombardy-Venetia (**c**), Venezia Giulia and Fiume (**d**) can provide an absorbing study involving issues under Italy and Austria. All this is fairly unpopular and therefore not over-expensive. The modern communist issues (**3a**), as might be expected, are more West-orientated than most, and some are even printed in Switzerland (**92c**).

Albania (**127a**) is almost as much a closed book to collectors as to travellers. The writer did for a time have a philatelic contact there, which ended abruptly when the Albanian wished to receive a rifle instead of a sending of stamps! The earlier issues are not only extremely scarce but also vulnerable to forgers (**e**), while the 'moderns' are thematic 'labels' of the worst kind (**f**).

Greece is popular throughout, her stamps ranging from expensive 'classics' (**a**) to the attractive multi-coloured present-day issues (**3d**). The very numerous island issues, coupled with the slightly unfamiliar alphabet, add to their fascination.

Bulgaria, **Roumania**, **Poland** and **Russia** can be considered together, though Poland did not have independent issues till after World War I. If the vast quantities of communist and thematic subjects are ignored, any of the four will be found full of other interest. Bulgaria (**b**) may be easiest in which to achieve any degree of completeness while Russia (**c**), as might be expected, offers something in every conceivable field of collecting, including stamps issued at various times in numerous subsidiary territories such as Estonia (**131g**), Azerbaijan (**d**) and the short-lived Far Eastern Republic (**e**).

Turkey too is a big country philatelically, particularly if one's interests extend over her entire former empire and to the many postal services established by other countries within her borders (**g**). Because of those her own earliest stamps were not much used, and those before 1929 have the drawback (or challenge) of inscriptions in the Arabic alphabet (**f**).

The **Arab** group, once mostly part of Turkey, can be roughly divided into five. First are the former French mandates of Syria and Lebanon (**a**) – at their inception not very different from French colonies but latterly fiercely independent in character. Then the one-time British mandates of Palestine (**b**), Iraq (**c**, **36b**), and Jordan (**27a**, **70b**) – all less popular than they were, but still an attractive if difficult group to collect. Next are the almost purely Arabic issues of Hejaz-Nejd (**136c**) (now Saudi-Arabia (**132a**)) and the Yemen (**132b**), which require some knowledge of the script and language to understand in detail. Fourth are the Gulf states of Qatar, Bahrain (**140a**) and Kuwait (**d**), to which may be added Aden (now South Yemen) (**75a**) – popular whilst their posts were run by India or Britain but now very much less so. Lastly come what are now the United Arab Emirates, a group of territories which for some years were used by agencies as scapegoats for incredible outpourings of thematic material, mostly without the remotest connections with Arab culture (**e**). Hardly one in ten thousand of these 'stamps' ever saw postal use, and they have probably done more harm to the cause of stamp collecting than any other factor – chiefly through the disillusionment of young people who buy them and then find they are virtually worthless.

SUGGESTED SUBJECTS AND TOPICS

Palestine issues were succeeded by those of **Israel** (**a**) which have a considerable following and are mostly within reach of the ordinary collector even if some of the unofficial end-of-mandate stamps are included for additional interest (**32e**).

Iran has fewer devotees than the range of her stamps would suggest, perhaps because of the number of reprints amongst her middle issues; a good showing and plenty of interest can be had at modest cost (**b**, **24b**). **Afghanistan**'s are much more primitive and mysterious; few people collect or understand them, so there are opportunities to find really scarce things – if one can – for very little cost (**c**, **d**). The 'earlies' of the so-called **Indian Native States** (**82b**, **136e**) are similar. Those of imperial **India** run parallel to British colonials and retain a following accordingly (**37a**, **71a**); but the unattractive issues that ensued in great profusion have little to recommend them except their cheapness (**e**). Many of the imperial issues were overprinted for the six so-called *Convention States* (**10**).

Ceylon, now **Sri Lanka** (**a**), had standard colonial issues (**21e**), beginning with classics (**22e**) only attainable by the connoisseur but otherwise fairly moderate in price and quantity. **Pakistan** (**b**) and **Burma** (**c**) are comparatively new countries in the stamp album – limited in scope but very collectable in conjunction with their Indian forerunners. The **Maldives** (**d**) have little to offer or commend, and **Bangladesh** and **Bhutan** even less, but **Nepal** (whose issues run from the 'Native States' era to the present day) (**136f**) or either **French** (**e**) or **Portuguese India** (**44a**) would provide interesting challenges to a collector wanting something off the beaten track.

China (**51b**) has many of the characteristics of Russia – 19th century imperial issues coupled with numerous locals, regional and revolutionary stamps in great numbers (**137a**), and modern communist series of the usual thematic and propaganda kinds (**24f**, **136g**). In addition, innumerable postal services set up by the European powers (**73d**, **132c**) and by Japan and the U.S.A. were in operation until as late as the 1920s and with their stamps provide another inexhaustible study. Language is a problem but Chinese stamps are fully catalogued and not hard to collect if one's net is not opened too wide. The issues of British **Hong Kong** (**97a**) are understandably more popular and more expensive; those of Portuguese **Macao** (**48f**) are likely to be harder to find but a good deal cheaper and hence an

156

attractive proposition to the beginner who wants something out of the common rut.

Few stamps of **Mongolia** (**156f**) have seen genuine postal use, the majority being what many collectors unkindly call 'wallpaper', and the same is true of North **Korea** (**137c**). South Korea, coupled with the former Korean empire, is little better known to most collectors (**137d**). Very many more turn to **Japan**, though the time is past when either her fascinating primitive 'earlies' (**a**) or even comparatively modern pictorials could be obtained very cheaply; there are resemblances to Switzerland here, and almost equal popularity (**b**, **93b**). Stamps of the **Ryukyus**, short-lived as a separate territory, are very similar (**137e**).

It is surprising that more do not collect the **Philippines**, which range from 19th century Spanish colonies (**c**), through the US era (**d**) (interrupted by Japanese occupation) to the present-day republican stamps (**e**) – nearly all of them in common everyday use. This is a country offering a great deal to those more interested in stamps *as* stamps than as an investment or a picture gallery.

Indo-China had a long period of French influence (**a**), followed by World War II occupations and the Viet-Nam period – sufficient indication that its stamps, including those of Laos (**97j**) and Kampuchea, are full of political complexities. **Thailand** is rather more straightforward, with a good deal of interest in the 19th century issues (**137f**), as well as attractive modern pictorials (**b**) – mostly European-printed throughout but with occasional local productions to add spice.

The Federation of **Malaysia** (**c**) is a large and interesting group with numerous threads running through it and some still continuing in the form of low-value series for fourteen individual states (**e, 52d**). One, **North Borneo** (now Sabah), has always been very popular because the chartered company which ran her affairs produced many series of finely engraved pictorials which have much increased in value (**25a**). **Sarawak**, rather similarly, had stamps portraying her white rajahs, the Brooke family (**d**). **Singapore**, once one of the **Straits Settlements** (**37g**) which formed a scattered British colony, is now independent and her well designed modern issues are in great demand (**122d**).

Indonesia, too, is a fascinating area, cheap at present (even if one includes most of the Dutch colonial issues (**141c**)) and likely to remain so (**a**). West Irian continued for a while, after general independence, as **Dutch New Guinea** (**b**); the other half of the same island, now the combined territory of **Papua New Guinea**, is high in collectors' esteem (**c**). So are the others under Australian influence: the Cocos Islands, Christmas and Norfolk Islands (**51c**) and the Australian Antarctic Territory. **Timor**, the formerly Portuguese half of another Indonesian island, is like Macao, a cheaper proposition but much more unpopular and difficult (**d**).

Australian stamps are at the height of their popularity – even those of the pre-Commonwealth states (**7a**, **21c**, **68d**) which remained so long in the doldrums – and can be recommended to those who can tolerate expensive-to-fill gaps alongside the cheaper issues (**37h**, **42c**, **53a**). **New Zealand** has always been popular throughout, with the exception of her too-numerous postal fiscals, postage dues and officials; there too a deep purse is needed (**2g**, **39d**, **139**).

STAMP COLLECTING

The **Pacific Islands** in general are very popular, but prices of the earlier and middle issues will deter many. The French territories of New Caledonia (**a**), Wallis & Futuna Islands and French Polynesia (**b**) would form an excellent field for the beginner; here it is mostly the 'moderns' which have risen in price. Tonga (**132e**) and the Cook Islands and their dependencies, once great favourites, have 'blotted their copybooks' with excesses of totally unnecessary issues, and should be avoided except by thematic collectors. Amongst the remainder Fiji (**c**) and the New Hebrides (now Vanuatu) have perhaps the most to offer, but new collectors may well prefer 'dead' territories like the 19th century kingdoms of Hawaii (**d**) and Samoa (**97d**), or newer ones like the Tokelau (**e**) or Pitcairn Islands (**f**) – unless or until their new issues become too prolific. There are others not mentioned above.

Canada is an expensive country if one attempts to start at the beginning, and particularly if one wants to include the early provincial issues (**g**). But a start in the 1930s (**141a**), or even in the present reign, will prove rewarding – whether a collection is made on simplified lines or whether it extends to postmarks, phosphor markings (**50b**), plate numbers and the like. Not all the provincials are expensive; a small representative showing of **Newfoundland (4a)** – stamps with a character entirely their own, which went on till 1949 – can be got together fairly readily. Nor ought the French islands of **St Pierre & Miquelon** to be overlooked: an unusual country which would provide pleasurable hunting for the patient collector.

USA stamps, not surprisingly, are extremely numerous and complex, especially the early (**h**) and middle issues with their innumerable varieties of watermark, perforation (**42b**, **43b**) and shade and the great number of official (**68c**), postage due, special delivery (**i**) and similar ancillary issues. Almost all are recess-printed, the design quality is high, and there are enough really common stamps for anyone to make a very substantial start before beginning to encounter cost problems. With few exceptions the stamps of the last forty years or more have increased very little in value – unlike the 'classic' issues which are widely regarded as a good investment provided they are in good condition.

Mexico (**24e**, **64e**) deters many people by her complexities of watermark (even amongst modern issues) and by her numerous revolutionary and provincial issues of 1913–15, but is well worth collecting on a simplified basis. Many of her designs are highly unconventional (**a**).

The **West Indies** can conveniently be looked at together, though very great differences exist. The former British colonies (which need not all be named here) were all favourites at one time (**71d**, **127c**) – and their pre-independence issues still are – but those which now promote vast numbers of new issues have put themselves near the bottom of the popularity chart – particularly Antigua (**2f**), Barbuda, Montserrat, Dominica, St Lucia (**b**), St Vincent, Grenada and the Grenadines. Amongst the more restrained can be included Bermuda (**70e**), which really lies much further north. The French islands of Guadeloupe and Martinique (**4e**), as well as French Guiana on the South American mainland, now use French stamps, which are well worth collecting with the appropriate postmarks along with the former distinct issues. The Netherlands Antilles are an attractive though not inexpensive group (**34**, **136a**) and so are the former Danish West Indies (**c**), now the US Virgin Islands. Porto Rico, now US territory too, had Spanish colonial issues, and so did **Cuba** (**64a**); the latter can now hardly be recommended except to those who hanker after 'thematic' material. That leaves the twin republics of **Haïti** and the

Dominican Republic (162d)– lumped in with Latin America by most people but each with her own philatelic character and with sufficient genuine outgoing mail to be very collectable.

Amongst the six **Central American** republics, Nicaragua (**37d, 60a–b**) and Panamá (**69a, 73e**) have ruined any chance of real popularity by far too great an output. With Nicaragua (**24a**), as well as El Salvador (**a**) and Honduras, the notorious agent Seebeck did business in the 1890s, providing stamps for their post offices' use and afterwards having them reprinted to his own requirements for sale to collectors. Even now the repercussions on the saleability of these countries' stamps can be felt. If one of this group is to be chosen, either Costa Rica, (**b**) or Guatemala (**70c**) will be found pleasing to collect though neither is cheap because of demand from the USA. The former Canal Zone (**c**) is popular there too. Belize (formerly British Honduras (**7d**)) has gone so far down the path of blatantly unnecessary issues as to to be unlikely to be seriously collected again.

It would be unfair to generalize about **South America**, for the range is so great. Brazil (**b**, **137h**) and Uruguay (**133a**) are the favourites amongst dedicated philatelists because of the absorbing interest of their 19th century issues. Chile's 'classics' closely resemble British colonials and her later issues are mostly modest enough to maintain a degree of popularity. Colombia's earlies (**a**), on the other hand, can be classed as 'primitives' and have their own circle of devotees. Ecuador's reputation suffered at the hands of Seebeck while Paraguay and, to a less extent, Uruguay have allowed their modern issues to be manipulated by speculators. In Latin America in general the activities of such people have had less real effect than is generally supposed (except perhaps to keep demand and hence prices low) and the genuine use of stamps from all these countries is so great that any or all of them offer rich rewards to collectors at all levels from beginners to advanced specialists. An attractive feature of many (Ecuador (**c**) and Uruguay (**22c–d**, **40b**, **57a–b**) are examples) is a continual alternation between the use of local printers and first-class European and US firms, while others (Brazil, Chile (**d**) and Peru for example) have developed very individual styles of design. A choice is hard to make amongst the bigger countries, but Argentina (**2c**, **68a**) or Venezuela (**6d**, **49d**, **94b**) would be worth consideration, or Bolivia (**37c**) amongst the less prolific. Too many new stamps from the Guianas – Suriname (**56e**) (formerly Dutch) and Guyana (formerly British) – have ruined their popularity.

The **Falkland Islands** (**25c**, **122b**) were probably the most-liked British territory in the stamp album even before the Argentine invasion, in spite of the fact that so many of its stamps are now beyond the average collector's reach. Close runners-up are the various **Antarctic** territories (**a**, **b**, **c**), as well as Tristan da Cunha, St Helena (**d**, **116**) and Ascension (**94e**). The **Azores** (**e**) and **Madeira**, which had separate stamps in the past, have resumed issuing them and are likely to be collected more as a result.

Africa, now comprising about 50 independent states, is still often thought of by collectors as a series of British (**a**), French (**b**), Belgian (**c**), Portuguese (**49a**), Spanish (**97i**) and one-time German (**135d**) territories and protectorates – with the exception of **Liberia** (**28b**) and **Ethiopia** (**126d**) whose issues might be compared respectively with Latin American and Iranian. To a surprising extent the colonial characteristics of African stamps survive, the transition to independence being in some cases hardly detectable (**d**). Where this is not so (Ghana [Gold Coast] (**e**)), Mozambique, Sierra Leone, Togo (**f**) and Equatorial Guinea for example) the rift meant an abrupt cessation of collectors' interest.

a   b   c

The number of amalgamations and unions, secessions and subdividings make Africa an increasingly complex area to understand historically. As an example, the territories of British Central Africa (**134e**) and the British South Africa Company (**134f**) became respectively Nyasaland and Rhodesia (**122a**). Rhodesia became the colonies of Northern and Southern Rhodesia, which later united into the Federation of Rhodesia and Nyasaland (**a**). That soon split up again, Nyasaland becoming Malaŵi, Northern Rhodesia becoming Zambia, and Southern becoming first plain Rhodesia (**b**) and then Zimbabwe. Much interest can be found in tracing such changes in the stamp issues throughout the continent, including of course those in the French and other spheres of influence. Local conflicts and temporary political changes like the Boer War (**95b**), the Italian invasion of Ethiopia (**133e**) and the ephemeral states of Biafra (**c**) and Katanga can all be studied and illustrated.

In contrast the territorially more stable countries like Gambia (**7c**), Tunisia (**a**) and Lesotho (Basutoland) (**b**) offer more straightforward listings, to which if one feels inclined can still be added such postal history as the Italian posts in Tunis and Cape of Good Hope stamps used in Basutoland (**c**). **South Africa**, though no longer in the Commonwealth, is still treated by many collectors as though she were (**2d**, **92a**); her stamps and those of South-west Africa have a particular interest for their bilingual pairs (**d**), and in addition to the pre-Union issues of the four provinces (**28a**) there are separate series for several 'homeland' territories within her borders.

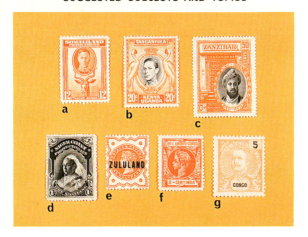

The issues of most of the European-colonized countries followed a fairly set pattern before independence, with certain exceptions, and there is no point in assessing every one here. Amongst the most popular with British collectors are, or were, Gambia, Mauritius (**33c**, **121b**), the Rhodesias, Nyasaland, Somaliland (**a**), Belgian Congo (**67d**) (now Zaïre), Kenya-Uganda-Tanganyika (**b**), and Zanzibar (**c**) (now part of Tanzania). The exceptions referred to are the chartered company territories, such as those of the British South Africa Company (Rhodesia, referred to above), the Mozambique (**4f**) and Nyassa Companies (**134c**), and the Niger Coast (**d**), all of which evolved their own stamp policies and created followings amongst collectors which tend to persist.

A few of the territories were very minor: for example Zululand (**e**) (British), Elobey, Annobon & Corisco (**f**) (Spanish) and Portuguese Congo (**g**), and most of their stamps are consequently scarce and expensive and hardly collectable except as adjuncts to the countries they are merged with.

Egypt (**140b**), and latterly **Sudan** (**a**), have been independent long enough for their more modern issues (**b**) to have swamped the considerable popularity these countries once enjoyed. **Morocco** is in a class of its own, its posts having for many years been operated by several European powers (**c**, **d**, **e**); their stamps with the 'forerunner' locals (**30d**) and the more recent independent issues (**18**) are a neglected but very collectable group. The French group has much more to offer than is generally realized, and Madagascar (**3c**), Réunion (**82a**, **134d**) (now using French stamps), Algeria (**79g**) (using French stamps till 1924) and the Ivory Coast (**f**) can perhaps be singled out for special interest.

171 a year's new issues from one country: Liechtenstein, 1983

From the above it will probably be realized that whatever countries are chosen, popular or unpopular, the collector has to make another choice – whether to collect new issues or, if not, at what point to draw a line. For even if he selects those with what is now regarded as a moderate output (Britain, for example, or Liechtenstein or Swaziland) he may find himself committed to an expenditure which would make it difficult to afford the older stamps – assuming, as is likely, that he finds them more interesting. If he commits himself to one with a policy of great numbers and/or high denominations he will quickly become disillusioned altogether with stamps and may be left with the feeling that his money would have been better used by a charity of his own choice.

172 a mixed set of unused and used: Nigeria, Silver Jubilee of King George V, 1935

There is also the much-discussed question of mint and used. A question often asked is 'which is more valuable, an unused stamp or a used one?' There is no general answer; used stamps of small countries and short-lived issues or little-used denominations of larger countries are naturally scarcer than unused, and may thus be worth more. Some collectors prefer unused (though they are more difficult to look after), while others maintain that only examples which have passed through the post are true stamps! Some try to collect both unused and used, while others indiscriminately keep either, not minding that a 'mixed' set is frowned on in the best circles!

173 France: part of a 'thematic' collection of views, arranged by Departments

It is probably clear by now that there are many more ways of collecting a country or group than by slavishly following a catalogue listing. One of these ways is postal history; another is the study in depth of printing methods; another, of more recent development, but without a very definite description, is the building up of a picture of a country by illustrating its history, landscape, natural history, industries, inventors, art etc. in whatever ways take one's fancy and with whatever stamps and postal material happen to be available. In this way it is possible to evolve a very personal collection which is never complete and yet may never appear incomplete, and which may become of equally absorbing interest to non-collectors. It may in fact aim to include all or most of the issued stamps, and some may need to appear more than once, to illustrate different subjects. It may even include appropriate stamps of other countries, but it is unlikely to fall prey to the excesses of those which issue constant streams of thematic series.

174 dealers' advertisements from a magazine

Something has been said in Chapter 6 about **thematic** collecting, with a *caveat* against embarking lightly on either an over-popular subject or an over-commercialized one. Indeed a glance through dealers' advertisements in any magazine is enough to suggest plenty of subjects *not* to collect; part of the fun of thematic collecting is, surely, to choose one's own subject and to treat it in one's personal way.

It is a good idea, once one has tasted general collecting for a period, and formed some conclusions as to which countries are of most interest, to take three choices: a group for building up in a general way, a single country or issue for some degree of 'specialization', and a 'theme' for a sideline album to be taken less seriously. Thus one might collect a group of, say, six or eight West African countries, and at the same time specialize in Barbados (perhaps as a result of having been there), and keep up a thematic collection of lighthouses. The possibilities are completely unlimited; that is one of the reasons for the hobby's popularity.

GLOSSARY

This list does not include printing terms, which are dealt with in Chapter 5, nor the different classes of stamp, described in Chapter 4.

Adhesive   A gummed stamp for attachment to an envelope, as distinct from the stamps impressed directly on to Postal Stationery.

Bisect   A stamp cut in halves and authorized for use at a proportion of its original value (**44b**).

Block   A group of stamps unseparated from one another, sufficient in size to show an intersection of the perforations (**39a–b**).

Bogus   A stamp pretended to have been issued but which never was. Sometimes the country-name is either fictional or that of an uninhabited island.

Cachet   A marking (often a 'rubber-stamp') applied to an envelope, usually to denote that it has travelled on a particular route; used extensively on air mails.

Cancellation   A method of preventing the re-use of a stamp; usually a postmark but sometimes a revenue mark; it may also be a pen-marking or even the removal of a small piece of the stamp.

Cancelled-to-order   Also written 'CTO'. Cancelled to satisfy a collectors' demand for used copies and sometimes (though not necessarily) sold more cheaply than unused. Stamps so cancelled are not always distinguishable from postally used (**25a–b**).

Chalk-surfaced paper   Paper specially treated to receive a good printing impression and to resist the removal of cancellations.

Comb perforation   A common method of perforation by a machine that treats each row of stamps in a sheet in turn, perforating the tops and sides and moving downwards after each stroke. Stamps when separated have regular corners (**38a, 39a**). A harrow machine goes further and perforates several rows at a time. (Cf. Line perforation.)

Compound perforation   Perforation with two different machines, often producing different gauges of hole on adjacent sides of a stamp (**39c**).

Control   Any marking that helps in the checking of counting and distribution. Examples are sheet serial numbers on the backs of stamps, dates in sheet margins, and overprints added to prevent the use of stolen stocks.

Cover   An envelope or other outer wrapping that has passed through the post. Pre-stamp and early stamped covers have postal markings, often of great value to historians.

Definitive   A stamp intended to remain in everyday use for a considerable period, as distinct from a provisional, commemorative or other special issue.

Die   The original single engraved piece of metal from which a multiple printing plate is built up.

Error   Any kind of mistake in production, such as an inverted centre, a wrong watermark, or a lack of perforations in an issue meant to be perforated. (Cf. Variety.)

Essay   A trial design. The term is usually applied to a printer's impression of a design not adopted for use (**56a–b**).

Face value   The price inscribed on a stamp to show its value for postage, as distinct from its catalogue value of market value.

Fake   A stamp manipulated to change its appearance, usually to deceive collectors (**21c**). (Cf. Forgery.)

First day cover   An example of a stamp or stamps used on a complete envelope on the first day of issue; often abbreviated to FDC (**18**).

Forgery   An imitation of a stamp, overprint or cancellation, intended to deceive either the post office (Postal Forgery) or collectors (**22b, d**).

Granite paper   Paper containing small flecks of coloured fibre as a security against forgery (**48d**).

Imperforate   Without perforations and separated by scissors or by tearing. A single imperforate stamp has edges more or less straight.

Imprint   The name of the artist, engraver or printer, often in the margin of either a stamp or a sheet (**43c**).

Line perforation   A method of perforation by a machine that punches the vertical and the horizontal lines of holes across the sheet at separate operations. Stamps when separated have irregular corners (**38b, 39b**). (Cf. Comb perforation.)

Local   A stamp authorized for use only within a limited territory (**30, 31**).

Maximum card   A postcard contrived to include the maximum number of allusions to a subject, e.g. by repeating a view depicted on the stamp and by being postmarked at the place concerned (**19**).

Miniature sheet   A small souvenir sheet containing one or more stamps, produced solely for collectors though valid for postage (**26, 29**).

Mint   In unused state as originally sold. Collectors usually allow a lightly mounted unused stamp to qualify as mint.

Obsolete   No longer on sale at post offices. Obsolete stamps must be *demonetized* before being invalid for postage.

O.G.   Abbreviation for Original Gum; applied principally to older stamps which may not be strictly 'mint' but yet retain most of their gum and general freshness.

Overprint   An additional printing (usually wording) applied to a stamp after its original production (**70e, 170c**). (Cf. Surcharge.)

Pane   A block of stamps forming a subdivision of a sheet.

Paquebot mail   Mail posted on a ship; often marked 'Paquebot' with a handstamp, and/or cancelled at a port foreign to the country whose stamps it bears (**75b**).

Perforations   The rows of punched holes separating stamps from one another in a sheet. Collectors distinguish different *gauges* of perforation (which denote the use of different machines) by reckoning the number of holes in a length of 2 centimetres by means of a special gauge. A stamp described as 'Perf. 15 × 14' has a gauge of 15 at top and bottom and 14 at the sides (**41**).

Postmark   Any marking made by postal authorities on a letter, by machine, handstamp or pen; particularly the cancellation on a stamp.

Pre-cancel   A stamp cancelled before sale with a distinctive marking, generally for use on bulk postings of printed matter (**66d–f**).

Proof   A trial printing from a die or plate, either finished or at an intermediate stage in its manufacture (**56e, 57a**).

Provisional   A stamp in temporary use (**63a–d**).

Re-entry   A partial or complete doubling of engraved lines due to a design having been impressed twice on to the printing plate.

Remainder   A stamp sold off after becoming obsolete, sometimes at below face value, instead of being destroyed (**24g**).

Reprint   A stamp reprinted to satisfy a demand from collectors, often distinguishable from the originals by paper, ink, etc (**24a–f**).

Rouletting   A method of separating stamps by means of *cuts* in the paper (**40**). (Cf. Perforations which are *holes*.)

Self-adhesive   A stamp with a permanently sticky back, protected before use by a removable piece of paper (**51c**).

Series or **set**   A group of stamps of similar design and purpose, usually issued and used at one period (**116**).

Se-tenant   Joined together. The term is applied to stamps of different design printed together (**34, 35c**), often for booklets.

Specimen   An example; usually one intended for circulation to member countries of the UPU and marked 'Specimen' or its equivalent (**58b–c**).

Strip   A single row or column of three or more stamps joined together (**35c**). (Cf. Block.)

Surcharge   An overprint which confirms or changes the face value of a stamp (**60a, b, c, e**).

Tête-bêche   Inverted in relation to one another (**35a–b**).

Unused   Not cancelled, but not necessarily in mint condition.

Used   Cancelled, usually to denote having done postal duty.

Variety   Any kind of distinctive feature, e.g. of perforation, watermark or design detail, which may warrant collecting separately from the normal; not necessarily an error.

Vignette   The centre picture of a two-coloured stamp, faded away in tone at its edges so as to allow for variation in register when printing (**169b–c**). The term is also sometimes applied to blue air mail labels (**63e**).

Watermark   The semi-transparent design impressed in paper during manufacture.